THE
WAINSCOTT
WEASEL

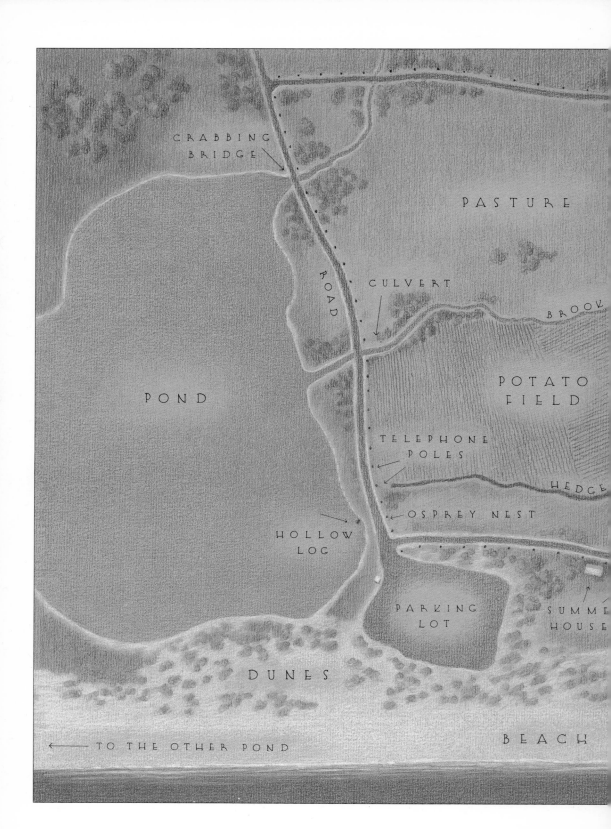

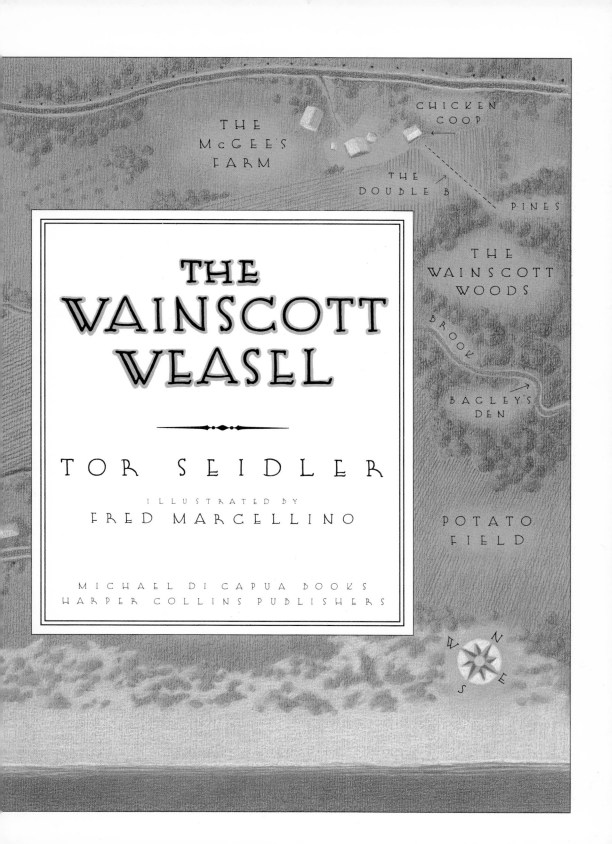

THE
McGEE'S
FARM

CHICKEN
COOP

THE
DOUBLE B

PINES

THE
WAINSCOTT
WOODS

BROOK

BAGLEY'S
DEN

POTATO
FIELD

THE WAINSCOTT WEASEL

TOR SEIDLER

ILLUSTRATED BY
FRED MARCELLINO

MICHAEL DI CAPUA BOOKS
HARPER COLLINS PUBLISHERS

For Jean Burch Falls

THE WAINSCOTT WEASEL

THE WAINSCOTT WOODS

Most weasels have to devote nearly all their waking hours to hunting—but not in Wainscott. In Wainscott, weasels are blessed with free time. During the winter these lucky creatures take a lot of long naps. Once the weather warms up, they dance.

Wainscott used to be about the sleepiest spot on the South Fork of Long Island. A few farms, some woods, and the beach—that was it. But thanks to what human beings call "development," the farms have been shrinking, their fields gobbled up by summer houses. The woods have shrunk, too, for the same reason. Still, the Wainscott woods haven't disappeared completely. And tucked away in the middle of the scrub oaks there remains a fine old stand of pines. These pines are forever shedding their needles, and the needles make the ground an excellent dance floor: slick as can be, perfect for sliding and gliding.

Since dancing is ridiculous without music, the weasels' dance season didn't usually start till May, when the songbirds fly in from the south. But one year the warm weather and the birds arrived a month early. So the weasels were able to have their First Spring Cotillion in April.

After a winter without dancing, the first cotillion was always an irresistible event, and this year, as usual, weasels from the newer Wainscott families arrived under the pines early, before four o'clock. They squealed happily along with the birds, pounding the needles with their paws. Weasels from the older families arrived later and stood around talking quietly among themselves. But even they couldn't keep their eyes from shining and their tails from twitching.

Of all the weasels under the pines on that warm April afternoon, the noisiest and most rambunctious were probably the five Whitebelly brothers. The Whitebellys were strapping young weasels with blazing white underbellies. The oldest, and strappingest, was Zeke. Zeke was the best dancer, too. In fact, he tended to be a bit of a show-off. If there was a lull in the music, for example, he would do a back flip. But he could twirl a pretty young weasel till her head spun.

The two weasels Zeke had most enjoyed twirling last season were both, it so happened, at the First Spring Cotillion. This was nice, in a way, but in another way it made Zeke's life complicated. Dancing with Sally Spots was fun, but while he was out on the needles with her, it was hard not to notice the scowl on Mary Lou Silverface's pale, pretty face. And as soon as he switched to Mary Lou, Sally crossed her forepaws and marched away.

After a while Zeke excused himself from Mary Lou and joined his brothers at the edge of the needles. "Benny boy," he said. "Be a pal and ask Sally to dance, will you?"

"Sure thing, Zeke," said Ben, the second-oldest Whitebelly. "Where is she?"

"I think she's over behind—"

Behind the big stump, Zeke was about to say, but his jaw had dropped. Seated on a root of the stump were the Blackishes, one of the grandest weasel couples in Wainscott. Standing beside them was a young weasel with radiant black fur, miraculously close-set, sparkly eyes, and a blue-jay feather tucked behind one ear.

"Who's she?" Zeke asked, gaping.

"Search me," said Ben.

Zeke turned to his brother Bill.

"Search me," Bill said.

"Search us, too," said the two youngest Whitebellys, who were twins.

Just then Mary Lou drifted over. "Zee-eeke," she whined. "I thought we were dancing."

Zeke didn't seem to hear her.

"Hey, Zeke," Ben said, elbowing him. "Mary Lou's talking to you."

"Huh?"

"Mary Lou's talking to you."

But by then Mary Lou had seen what Zeke was gawking at. She turned and stomped off.

"Jeez," Zeke said. "Go ask her to dance, will you, Ben?"

"But you just told me to ask Sally."

"Oh, yeah. Billy, you go ask Mary Lou. Okay?"

"Anything you say, Zeke," said Bill.

"How about us?" chimed the twins.

"You boys keep your tails crossed for me," Zeke said.

5

The Blackishes had been in Wainscott far longer than the Whitebellys, but this didn't keep Zeke from sauntering straight over to them. "Hiya, Mr. and Mrs. Blackish," he said. "Great cotillion weather, huh?"

"Lovely," said Mrs. Blackish. "And to think it's only April!"

"I don't like it," Mr. Blackish grumbled. "This heat keeps up and the woods'll be a tinderbox by July." Mr. Blackish didn't much like this Whitebelly, either. The brash young weasel hadn't so much as tipped his cap to him and his wife.

"Hi," Zeke said, smiling at the gorgeous stranger. "Zeke Whitebelly."

"My niece, Wendy Blackish," Mrs. Blackish said. "She's down from the North Fork for the season."

Zeke's eyes lit up. He was still young enough for a season to seem like forever. "Great feather, Wendy," he said. "Are they big up there?"

"Actually, I just found it this morning," Wendy confessed, her snout blushing a little.

"How do you like Wainscott?" Zeke asked.

"Oh, I love it!" she said. "The sea breezes, the eggs, all the free time . . . It's heaven!"

"You don't have free time and eggs up there on the North Fork?"

They certainly didn't—any more than they had weasels as handsome and muscular as this Zeke. "We don't have a Double B," Wendy explained, trying not to stare at Zeke's fine white belly.

"So, you like our eggs," Zeke said with a grin. "Me and my brothers do Double B duty all the time."

The Double B was famous even up on the North Fork. It was a remarkable tunnel that ran the quarter mile from the edge of the Wainscott woods to the chicken coop on the McGees' farm.

"Is it dark inside?" Wendy asked.

"You bet," Zeke said. "It's black as a crow in there."

"It must be hard work, rolling eggs."

"Mm," Zeke said, flexing his muscles.

"And the farmer never misses them?"

"We've got a system. We go at dawn, before Mrs. McGee comes to collect the eggs, and we never touch a feather on the chickens—yummy as they look. There's zillions of them, and they lay eggs like it's going out of style, but we never take more than a few dozen—just enough to feed us."

"Hm," Wendy said. "Does the Wainscott weasel's son roll eggs, too?"

"The *who*?"

"The Wainscott weasel's son."

"What do you mean?" Zeke said, frowning. "We're all Wainscott weasels around here."

"She means Bagley Brown," Mrs. Blackish said.

"Up on the North Fork he's just called the Wainscott weasel," Wendy explained. "He's the only one anybody's heard of. I've been here a whole week and I still haven't seen his son yet."

"Young Bagley doesn't socialize much," Mrs. Blackish said.

Mr. Blackish humphed. "I told you I'd introduce you as soon as our paths cross, Wendy. I knew his father well."

Mr. Blackish always held his head high, but as he spoke of his acquaintance with Bagley Brown, his nose rose a notch higher. Bagley Brown was the greatest name in all weaseldom —revered far and wide. It was he who was responsible for the wondrous Double B. In fact, Double B stood for Bagley Brown. The great weasel was now dead. Or so weasels said. His body had never actually been found, and some believed he'd simply gone off in search of new challenges. In either case, his legend burned as brilliantly as ever, and since the moment of her arrival in Wainscott, Wendy had been dying to catch a glimpse of his son, Bagley Brown Jr. In fact, Bagley Jr. was the reason she'd stuck the feather behind her ear. She'd assumed he would be at the cotillion. But so far there was no sign of him.

"Bagley rolls eggs sometimes," Zeke told her. "But not as much as me. And he dances like an old groundhog."

"How would you know?" Mr. Blackish said.

"You've got to see well to dance," Zeke said. "Specially if you throw in flips. But Bagley always has to wear that stupid eye patch of his, to set himself apart."

"Doesn't he have a bad eye?" Wendy asked.

"Nah. He only started wearing it after his father died."

"It's a mark of mourning," Mr. Blackish said. "And even if it is a bit of an affectation, it's hardly for the likes of you to question it."

"What's an affectation, Uncle?" Wendy asked.

"Oh, it means . . . putting on airs a bit. Heaven knows, he deserves to be set apart—out of respect for his father. And as far as dancing goes, I suspect he just doesn't care for it."

"But all young weasels like to dance," Zeke said.

"What do you mean?" said Wendy. "I've never danced in my life."

"You're kidding!"

She shook her head. "This is the first dance I've ever been to."

"Then it's about time you got out on the needles," Zeke said, extending a paw.

Wendy felt a pleasant whir of excitement. "But I don't know how," she said.

"I'll show you. Anyhow, all weasels can dance. It's in our blood."

"Well . . . Is it all right?"

Mr. Blackish looked less than thrilled at the idea of his niece dancing with an upstart weasel who didn't even tip his cap.

But Mrs. Blackish smiled and said, "Go ahead, dear." So Zeke led Wendy out onto the dance floor.

At that moment the beat was quick. A couple of catbirds were really going at it up in the pines. But as Zeke said, all weasels can dance, and in no time Wendy was whirling around as if she'd been doing it all her life. Mary Lou Silverface, who was dancing with Zeke's brother Bill, shot her a pitch-dark look, as did Sally Spots, who was dancing with Ben. But Wendy didn't notice. She was too busy trying not to stare at Zeke's handsome belly. When he suddenly did a back flip, her heart did one, too.

But after a while she began to feel a little flushed. "Thank you, Zeke," she said, stopping.

Zeke looked around. Mr. and Mrs. Blackish were no longer by the stump. "You're a real natural, Wendy," he said, leading her back there.

"I was ghastly," she said happily. "But it is fun."

"Isn't it the best? We've got to do it again soon."

"Well . . . my aunt said something about a tea dance at the Tantails' on Sunday. Are you going to that?"

The Tantails were very exclusive and hadn't asked the Whitebellys. Normally Zeke wouldn't have minded a bit—at exclusive parties weasels always talked more than they danced—but just now he minded a lot. "I wasn't invited," he muttered.

Wendy gulped, afraid she'd been tactless. "Oh," she said. "Wait here a minute, will you?"

"Sure," Zeke said agreeably.

Wendy searched for her aunt and uncle behind the big stump, but all she found there was a rabbit, who turned his cottontail and fled. Wendy climbed the stump. From on top of it, she spotted her aunt and uncle chatting with a pair of elderly weasels on the other side of the dance floor. She climbed back down and walked over to them.

The way her uncle sniffed at the sight of her made her suspect she'd worked up a musky odor on the dance floor. She would have to take a quick bath in the brook.

After being introduced to the elderly couple, she drew her aunt aside. "Don't you have an extra invitation to that tea dance on Sunday, Aunt?"

Mrs. Blackish laughed softly. "I suppose you have someone in mind?"

"Well . . ."

"It's at home. Just inside the front entrance." She smiled. "He *is* quite a dancer, dear."

Wendy had always been quick on her paws, and it took her only a couple of minutes to get back to the Blackishes' lovely old den. The invitation was just inside, as her aunt had said. It was a scrap of paper stamped with Mrs. Tantail's left front pawprint in aged wineberry juice. Holding a corner of it between her teeth, Wendy hurried off to the brook for a quick bath.

In spite of the warm weather, the oak trees weren't fully leafed out yet, so she kept to the underbrush in case a hawk was circling overhead. As she popped out of some brambles, she bumped right into another weasel.

"I'm so sorry!" she said, the invitation falling from her mouth.

"Is there a fox on your tail?" said the other, stepping between her and the brambles to protect her.

"Oh, no, I was just . . . just . . ."

Her voice died away. The stranger had turned from the brambles to her.

"Are you all right, miss?"

Wendy was not all right. She felt decidedly faint. The weasel standing before her had sleek brown fur and a patch over one eye.

THE POND

Wendy's eyes fluttered open. There, an inch or so away, was what was surely the face of Bagley Brown Jr. Realizing she'd passed out in his paws almost made her pass out again, in embarrassment.

"Are you all right?" he repeated.

She opened her mouth, but no sound came out.

"Can I get you something?" he asked.

"Bagley Brown," she said in wonder.

But then she remembered her odor and jerked away from him, looking around rather wildly for the brook. "The dancing must have gone to my head!" she said.

He picked up the invitation. "Looking for this?"

"Oh, thank you." But she didn't step forward to take it. "You—you are Bagley Brown Jr., aren't you?"

"Yes," he said, though without much enthusiasm. There was a strange sadness in his eye. "And you?" he asked. "You're not from Wainscott, are you?"

"I'm from the North Fork."

"The North Fork! How'd you get way down here?"

"The farmer who owns the land we live on delivers hay to a horse farm in Wainscott. I rode on his truck. We took two ferryboats. I got seasick."

"Sounds like a real experience. What made you leave home?"

"Well, it's kind of a long story. Things aren't so easy up there. We don't have . . ." But how could she bring out "Double B" in front of Bagley Brown Jr.! "My parents—my parents thought I might have a better life here," she stammered on. "I have an aunt and uncle in Wainscott, you see. To tell you the truth, I think my parents are hoping I'll find a husband down here."

"I shouldn't think you'd have much trouble with that," Bagley said. "Who are your aunt and uncle?"

"The Blackishes."

"Ah."

"I'm Wendy Blackish."

"Nice to meet you, Wendy. I like your feather."

"Thank you," she said, resolving to wear it always.

He smiled at her. "It's made of snakeskin," he said.

"My feather?"

"My patch. You were staring at it."

"Oh, no! I mean, I like it." Even if it was a bit show-offy, the patch seemed awfully romantic.

"Thank you," he said, holding out the invitation.

She took it and quickly backed up again. "Isn't the brook nearby?" she asked.

"You feel like a swim?"

"A swim, yes." It certainly sounded better than "a bath."

"Would you like to see something better than the brook?"

"Why . . . I guess so."

Just like that, the sadness in his eye evaporated. "Come with me, Miss Blackish," he said.

As they trotted off, her paws hardly felt the pebbles and twigs on the forest floor. What a remarkable place Wainscott was! One minute she was her plain old self, the next she was off on an adventure with the dashing son of Bagley Brown! He lived up to all her expectations, too. He was so polite and well-spoken, and the way he'd stepped up to face the fox— even though there hadn't been one—showed his courage.

But when they reached the edge of the woods, he seemed to become nervous.

"A hawk?" she said, watching him check the sky.

"No, all clear. Let's go."

It wasn't far from the edge of the woods to a hedge, but he sprinted across the open space as if afraid of being picked off from above. She followed at a less desperate pace, feeling slightly confused. Weren't foxes just as dangerous as hawks? But then, things in the sky might be harder to judge, distance-wise, with a patch over one eye.

Soon they were moving safely along under the hedge.

"Do you remember your father well?" she asked curiously.

"Very well."

"And the Double B? Were you around when he dug that?"

"I was around for the second tunnel. Though of course he didn't dig either one himself."

Weasels are not great diggers. Usually they don't even dig their own dens, preferring to take over burrows dug by other animals. So a quarter-mile-long tunnel would have been out of the question.

"I know, he got moles to do it," Wendy said. "He paid them back with a map of all the vegetable gardens in Wainscott, right?"

"He scratched it out on a piece of birch bark. It's their sacred treasure. Moles don't see too well above ground, you know."

"How'd he get them to dig the second tunnel?" The first one had caved in when a hurricane pounded Long Island with torrential rains.

"The map had improved the quality of their lives so much, they did it out of simple gratitude. And . . . I think they'd gotten kind of fond of my father, too."

There was a quiet pride in his voice when he spoke of his father that made Wendy like him even more. But suddenly she stopped and looked around. She'd been so busy asking questions she hadn't noticed the lawns and houses that had cropped up on either side of the hedge.

"Don't worry, they're just summer places," he told her. "The human beings aren't in them yet."

"Do they have cats?" she asked warily.

"Some. In the summer I usually go by the dunes."

"Cats don't like dunes?"

He just shrugged, as if cats concerned him no more than foxes.

"Do you ever hope . . ." she asked.

"Oh, dear," he said, giving her a sidelong look. "Do I seem completely hopeless?"

"Oh, no!" Bagley Brown Jr., hopeless! "I was only going to ask . . . Some weasels say your father just disappeared as soon as the second tunnel was finished. Do you ever hope he'll come back?"

He shook his head. "No," he murmured.

When they came to the end of the hedge, he led the way to a telephone pole at the side of a road. He looked both ways, then studied the sky again.

"All clear," he said.

He dashed across the pavement, but Wendy, who didn't care to lug the invitation in her mouth anymore, strolled across on her hind legs. The pavement was pleasantly warm.

She joined him in some tall reeds and cattails on the other side. As they weaved their way through the stalks, her nose

began to twitch. She smelled water. And in a few yards the
reeds gave way to a narrow strip of sand: the shore of an
enormous pond. She could hear a faint roar, but there wasn't a
breath of wind, and the water was perfectly still—a huge mirror
reflecting the soft blue of the twilight sky. Floating in the middle of the pond was a pair of swans, whiter than a weasel's
winter coat. Circling high overhead were half a dozen sea gulls.

"Better than the brook?" Bagley asked.

"Oh, it's absolutely beautiful!"

"The ocean's just beyond that spit of sand. Listen. You can
hear the waves."

That was the muffled roar.

"It's safe to swim here?" she asked.

"Sure. You can go right through that log."

A hollow log stuck straight out over the pond like a pier.

"Will you hold this?" she said.

He took the invitation, and she stuck her feather in the sand
and crawled into one end of the log. The other end rested on
a rock out in the pond, so the opening was above water level.
From there she lowered herself in.

Weasels aren't great swimmers, but they enjoy a dip now
and then. And though it was only April, the pond wasn't too
chilly. Wendy splashed around merrily. But while washing
off, she remembered how she'd worked up an odor in the first
place. Dancing. She'd been so carried away with Bagley Brown
Jr. she'd totally forgotten about Zeke Whitebelly!

She swam straight to shore and shook herself dry.

"I'm afraid I have to be getting back," she said. "I just cross
the road and follow the hedge back to the woods, right?"

"I'll take you."

"Don't be silly. I can find my way."

But awful as she felt about deserting Zeke, she could hardly stand to leave Bagley Brown. While looking into the edge of the pond to put her feather back behind her ear, she had an idea.

"Will you keep that?" she said, turning to him with a shy smile.

"What?"

"The invitation. It's for the Tantails' tea dance on Sunday. Or do you already have one?"

"If I got one, I probably tossed it out. I'm afraid I'm not much on dancing."

"But you wouldn't have to dance. It would just be so nice to see you again."

"Well . . . thank you, Wendy. I guess—I'd be glad to come. But I insist on walking you back to the woods."

She could tell he didn't really want to leave the pond, though. Every time he glanced at it, his eye took on a dreamy glaze. Besides, if he went back with her, he might come all the way to the pines, and if Zeke was still waiting, things could get sticky. It was going to be sticky enough explaining to Zeke that she couldn't get him an invitation to the tea dance.

"I really do feel like walking by myself, if you don't mind," she said.

"Well, I'll see you to the road, anyway."

He escorted her through the reeds and the rushes. At the road she looked both ways and crossed.

"See you Sunday, Bagley!" she cried, waving from the other side. "And thanks for showing me the lovely pond."

STEAMED

Zeke Whitebelly was leaning against the stump under the pines. He'd been waiting for Wendy such a long time that Sally Spots and Mary Lou Silverface, who were dancing with his brothers, had started to point at him and giggle. The slinky stranger he'd deserted them for had deserted him—just as he deserved!

Zeke was getting hot under his fur. It steamed him to be put in such a ridiculous position. And yet, oddly enough, he wasn't steamed at the weasel who'd put him in it. Somehow Wendy Blackish was too charming and gorgeous to get angry at. She'd asked him to wait by the stump, and wait there he would, no matter how much pointing and giggling he had to put up with.

Finally, when the dance was beginning to wind down, Wendy came racing back under the pines. She was breathless, and her coat was shinier than ever, as if she'd washed off.

"I'm *so* sorry to have kept you waiting all this time, Zeke," she said, coming straight up to him.

"No problem," he said with a grin. The thought that she'd spruced up just for him erased all his anger. She looked even prettier than before, if that was possible.

"The thing is . . . there wasn't an extra invitation. I looked and looked."

"That's okay. Tea dances aren't exactly my cup of tea, any-way—ha, ha." He glanced up into the pines. The daylight was dying, but the catbirds were still crooning away. "How about one more dance, Wendy?"

"That would be lovely."

Zeke didn't smirk at Sally or Mary Lou as he led Wendy out, but he did stand his tallest—which made him taller than any other weasel there. Soon he forgot about Sally and Mary Lou altogether, forgot about everyone except Wendy. Not only was she breathtakingly beautiful, she truly was a natural dancer. He felt as if the pine needles had fallen there, as if the birds were singing overhead, just for the two of them.

But as he swept her out to the edge of the needles, somebody grumbled. It was Mr. Blackish. He was tapping a hind paw impatiently on the ground.

"Uh-oh," Wendy said. "I guess I better go."

Zeke didn't feel a bit like stopping, but it was important to make a good impression on her relatives, so he led her over to them.

"About time," Mr. Blackish said.

"Whatever became of you, dear?" Mrs. Blackish wondered. "We lost track of you."

Wendy looked down.

"If we don't get out of here, we'll be the last to leave," Mr. Blackish said sourly. "Evening, Zach."

"Zeke," Zeke said.

"I take it we'll be seeing you on Sunday, Zeke," Mrs. Blackish said with a smile, trying to make up for her husband.

"'Fraid not, Mrs. Blackish. Wendy couldn't find an invite."

"But it was just inside the—" She stopped, seeing Wendy squirm.

"Yes, well, good-bye then," Mr. Blackish said.

With that, he gave his wife and niece a paw each and led them away. Wendy glanced over her shoulder, but she didn't call out good night or anything.

Left standing there alone, Zeke felt even more steamed than before. The invitation to the Tantails' clearly existed, and

Wendy knew it. Which meant she must have decided not to ask him. But that just didn't make sense. She'd been having such a good time dancing with him. She couldn't have been faking it. The only possible explanation was that she'd given the invitation to someone else while he was waiting for her by the stump.

He quickly rounded up his brothers, ignoring the cold shoulders he got from Sally and Mary Lou.

"You okay, Zeke?" Bill asked. "You look kind of mad."

Zeke snorted. "When I get my paws on that weasel, Billy boy, I'm going to pulverize him."

"What weasel?" asked Ben.

"Whoever weaseled the invite out of Wendy." Even now Zeke couldn't be mad at her.

"What invite?" chimed the twins.

"Some bash the Tantails are tossing next Sunday. Come on, boys."

The last stragglers were leaving the pines, heading for their dens. But the Whitebelly brothers didn't go home. They started marauding around the darkening woods, hoping to get their paws on a weasel with an invitation.

THE STRIPED FISH

After making sure Wendy was safely under the hedge across the road, Bagley Brown Jr. wound his way back through the reeds to the pond. He weighted the invitation down with a pawful of sand and slipped into the hollow log.

Crouched in the far end of the log, Bagley kept watch over the water. It wasn't as smooth as a few minutes ago, for now was the time of day when insects flocked to the pond. Swallows were swooping at them from above, while fish were trying to catch the poor bugs from below. Every time one of the feeding fish made a rip in the pond's silken fabric, Bagley felt a little rip inside his chest.

The sun was setting across the water. The sky turned rosy, and so did the pond. When the very top of the sun was about to sink below the horizon, Bagley poked his head out from the end of the log. A few feet away, a striped fish was drifting by. Bagley spat at it with all his might.

A dark wad landed in the water and gradually came apart, turning into four separate specks: four dead insects. Bagley had plucked them out of the spiderweb near his den that morning. They'd been stored in his cheek the whole time he'd been with Wendy. The fish came up almost to the surface, looked the bugs over, and daintily swallowed them, one by one. After the meal she made another pass in front of the log, giving Bagley a curious glance as she swam by. Then she disappeared into the depths.

Bagley stared after her for a long while. He'd first caught sight of her about a month ago, from this same log. He'd been coming to this log for ages. The pond had had a mysterious attraction for him ever since his father had showed it to him when he was little. And the hollow log, with its overhead protection, was the ideal spot for crouching and watching the magical way the land and the sky communicated through the pond's ever-changing surface. Even so, he never used to come more than once a week. Since spotting the striped fish, he'd come every day.

The first time, of course, he'd had no bugs in his cheek. He'd just been staring idly at some gnats buzzing over the water when all of a sudden something blinded him. He'd blinked. There, hanging in the air, was a fish, the sun striking off her lovely silver scales. She had dazzling eyes and glorious greenish stripes—and for a split second only her tail was in the water. Then she splashed back into the pond.

The sight left him spellbound. He'd never seen such a ravishing creature in his life. And soon her head broke the surface again, as if she was scouting for more gnats. Bagley moved to the brink of the log. Usually he didn't speak to strangers before they spoke to him. Striking up conversations led to exchanging names, and his name generally made a sensation and got him

special treatment—which he hated, since it was all because of his father, not him. But that day, without even thinking, he'd called out:

"Good afternoon!"

The fish had taken one look at him and sunk from sight. Bagley remained in the log till nightfall, but she never returned.

It was late when he'd gotten back to his den, and after a small supper he'd curled up to sleep. But as soon as he closed his eye, he saw the beautiful fish. He tried to blink the image away. A weasel had no business mooning over a fish. They didn't even live in the same element. He lived on land, she lived in the water.

After promising himself to put the striped fish out of his mind, he'd finally dozed off. But the fish simply glided into his dreams. Worse, she was the very first thing he thought of when he woke up the next morning. He clenched his teeth and reminded himself he was a weasel, with four legs and a fine coat of fur, not a creature with scales and no legs at all. And yet every time the sleek, silvery, green-striped fish swam into his mind, a tingling ran down his spine all the way to the tip of his tail. Why should a fish seem beautiful to him? Was it perhaps because he saw things through just one eye? Whatever the reason, he was fighting a losing battle with himself, and by the end of that day he surrendered and returned to the pond.

The fish had been feeding when he got there. He'd crouched at the end of the hollow log, waiting, and just before dark he'd caught sight of the striped fish, coasting along just under the water, a few feet away from him. But she never broke the surface. It was still early in the spring, and there weren't all that many bugs out.

He'd thought about bugs on the way back to his den, which was on the bank of the brook that wound through the Wainscott woods. This brook was spring-fed, so it never ran dry, and Bagley's father had chosen to live there in order to have a handy and dependable water supply. The nearest neighbors were a pair of spiders who had cleverly constructed their web between two branches of a tree limb that had fallen across the brook. Bugs spawned in and around the brook, so the web always trapped twice as many as the spiders could eat.

Still, the spiders were horrified the morning Bagley Jr. walked out onto the limb and started looking over their bugs.

"May I take a few?" he asked.

Neither spider had ever heard of a weasel liking bugs, but they were deeply relieved that he bothered to ask, since he could easily have cleaned out the web without their permission. They invited him to take a few bugs whenever he liked.

"Though we'd appreciate it," one of them added, "if you wouldn't damage the web."

Bagley had removed three bugs with great care and, later in the day, carried them to the pond in his cheek. He'd waited at the end of the log. When the striped fish eventually swam by, he spat the bugs in her direction. She vanished into the deep water with a flick of her tail. But it wasn't too long before she returned. She poked the floating bugs a few times with her pretty snout, then swallowed them, one by one. Since that time, Bagley had brought bugs for her every day, and she would often peer up at him before gliding off into the mysterious depths of the pond—just as she had this evening.

Once the last glow of the sunset died away, Bagley shuffled back out through the log. But as he was about to head into the reeds, he felt something under one of his paws. There, in the sand, was the invitation to the Tantails' tea dance.

He felt discouraged. He'd completely forgotten about Wendy Blackish. Here he'd met a pretty, spirited young weasel, one who seemed to like him, and all he'd been thinking of for the last hour was a fish!

"You're a sick weasel, Bagley Brown," he muttered, picking the invitation up.

FIVE AGAINST ONE

When Bagley felt the sandy shoulder of the road under his paws, his heart started pounding against his rib cage. He tried to calm himself, but it was no use. There weren't any headlights coming down the road. The only source of light was a smattering of stars in the moonless sky.

After examining the sky for a long time, he put the invitation in his mouth and darted across to the telephone pole. Once he was under the hedge, the pounding in his chest stopped. But as soon as he got to the other end of the hedge, his heartbeat took off again. It was almost impossible to tell what was up above, the stars shed so little light.

As he was about to sprint across the open space to the woods, he heard a whooshing sound and froze. He didn't budge till the moon rose. Then, with visibility improved, he realized the whooshing was only the wind in the hedge. He swallowed hard and bolted for the trees.

"What's wrong, Bagley?" someone said as he came hurtling into the woods.

Bagley stopped by the trunk of an oak and looked around. There in the glimmering moonlight were the five Whitebelly brothers.

"Sky-scared?" asked the biggest of them, grinning.

Bagley took the invitation out of his mouth to speak but didn't deny the accusation. He just said, "Good evening, Zeke."

"What's that?" Zeke demanded.

"This? An invitation to a tea dance at the Tantails'. Why?"

"Where'd you get it?"

"What business is that of yours?" Bagley asked, leaning back against the oak. He wasn't used to being grilled.

"Just a friendly question."

"Hm. Well, I got it from the Blackishes' niece, Wendy."

"That right?" Zeke said, stepping closer.

In spite of what he'd said about Bagley's dancing, Zeke had as much respect for the name Bagley Brown as any other weasel. Not that Zeke was any good at bowing and scraping; but normally, when he ran into Bagley, he was extra polite. This time was different, though. He was steamed. By all rights, that invitation was *his*.

"You wanted to see my new left-right combination, didn't you, Benny boy?" he said. "Well, get a load of this."

Zeke outweighed Bagley by several ounces, but when Zeke swaggered up to him, Bagley stood his ground, his heartbeat hardly quickening at all. And just as Zeke tried to demonstrate his left-right combination, Bagley ducked—so instead of Bagley's jaw, Zeke hit the rock-hard bark of the oak tree.

Zeke doubled over in pain. But his brother Ben instantly took his place. Ben was just Bagley's size. Backpedaling away from the tree, Bagley dodged Ben's punches. Ben got frustrated and made a dive for him. Bagley sidestepped, and Ben landed on his face, skinning his snout on a rock.

While Ben lay there whimpering, up stepped Bill. Bill wasn't the brightest of the Whitebelly bunch, and he was a bit smaller than Bagley, but he was eager to prove himself and actually made Bagley gasp with a paw to the gut. Not a violent weasel by nature, Bagley couldn't help cuffing Bill hard across his left ear.

As Bill staggered away, dazed, the twins stepped up and made their paws into fists. But strapping as they were for their age, they weren't full-grown yet. What's more, they'd heard the name Bagley Brown spoken with awe all their short lives. So when Bagley told them to look after their brother Bill, they immediately obeyed him.

By now Zeke was ready for another round. He'd never been so furious in his life. "You've had it, Bagley Brown," he snarled.

"What's this all about, Zeke?" Bagley asked. "What do you want from me?"

"That," Zeke said, pointing at the invitation on the ground.

"Is that all?" Bagley picked it up. "Why didn't you say so?"

Zeke blinked in surprise. "You mean I can have it?"

"I don't see why not."

Bagley hadn't really wanted to go to the tea dance anyway. It didn't seem right to lead Wendy on, considering his feelings for the striped fish. Besides, if he decided he wanted to go, he wouldn't need an invitation. His name made him welcome anywhere, anytime.

"She's nice, that Wendy—and very pretty," he said, handing the invitation to the amazed Zeke. "You two would make a great couple."

For about the first time in his life Zeke was speechless. It took him fully half a minute to find his voice.

"Gosh, Bagley, you're aces," he said at last. "If there's ever anything I can do for you—and I mean *anything*—you just holler. Okay?"

"Can you get me some gills and some fins?"

"What?"

"Just a joke. You guys want to come over for an egg? You could wash off that scrape on your snout, Ben."

Ben made a sour face. He was mad at himself for whimpering. But Zeke said, "Great," and as soon as Bill recovered from his dizziness, they all trooped off to Bagley's den by the brook.

THE TEA DANCE

Ｉt got warmer and warmer as the week went by, and Sunday felt less like spring than a lazy summer day. But the heat didn't make Wendy lazy. She kept bouncing from her nook in the Blackishes' den to her aunt and uncle's, to ask her aunt how she looked. She changed her fur style again and again, and switched the feather from one ear to the other and then back.

"I think you should calm down, dear," Mrs. Blackish advised her. "It's just a tea dance."

"But I've never been to a tea dance before."

"It won't be that different from the cotillion, dear. Only not so many weasels. And you really shouldn't get your hopes up about Bagley Brown." On their way home from the cotillion Wendy had explained to her aunt and uncle what had become of the extra invitation from the Tantails.

"I'm sure he'll come, Aunt. He said he'd be glad to."

"But I don't remember ever seeing him at a dance before. He's almost . . . well, he's almost antisocial."

"Let's wait and see, shall we?" said Mr. Blackish. He'd praised Wendy's judgment in giving the invitation to Bagley instead of Zeke. "He might make an exception for Wendy. That would be quite a catch, I must say—Bagley Brown Jr."

Wendy couldn't help smiling at the idea. "Hadn't we better go, Uncle? I'm sure it's four by now."

"Well-bred weasels never arrive on time," Mr. Blackish told her.

So Wendy had to control her nerves for another half hour. And once they started for the pines, she kept getting ahead of her aunt and uncle and had to bite her tongue not to pester them to hurry up. But at last they arrived.

They certainly weren't early. Dozens of weasels were already gathered on the sun-dappled pine needles. But not one of them had an eye patch.

"I suppose Bagley Brown would be *really* late, Uncle?" Wendy said hopefully.

"Naturally," Mr. Blackish replied. "Come along, I'll introduce you to our hosts."

The Tantails, a childless, middle-aged couple, made a great fuss over Wendy. After a while Mrs. Tantail took Wendy aside to hear all about her trip from the North Fork. In the middle of her story, Zeke Whitebelly sauntered up to them.

"Zeke!" Wendy exclaimed.

"Hiya, Wendy," Zeke said. "Great weather for a tea dance, huh, Mrs. Tantail?"

Mrs. Tantail looked a bit blank. "Do I, er . . ."

"Zeke Whitebelly," Zeke said, producing an invitation.

"Oh. How—how kind of you to come."

"Thanks," Zeke said. "How you been, Wendy?"

"Fine," Wendy said. Surprised as she was, she found herself rather pleased to see the handsome weasel. She hadn't laid eyes on him since the cotillion.

"The birds are really cranked up today," he remarked. "I could get the dancing going, if you want, Mrs. Tantail."

"Um, well, if you feel like dancing . . ."

"I mean, you do dance at these tea dances, don't you, ma'am?"

"Well, I suppose, if one feels like dancing . . ."

"Great! How about it, Wendy?"

Wendy looked around. There was still no sign of Bagley Brown. And the birds really were singing up a storm. "Well, I guess," she said.

"Catch you later, Mrs. T.," Zeke said, taking Wendy by the paw. As he led her away, he said softly, "Good to see you again, Wendy."

"It's good to see you, too, Zeke. I'm glad they sent you an invitation after all."

"Well, to tell you the truth, they didn't."

"How'd you get it, then?"

"Bagley Brown gave it to me."

Wendy stopped abruptly. "What?"

"Bagley Brown gave it to me."

As this news sank in, Wendy trembled with mortification. She'd presented Bagley with the invitation, and he'd just turned around and given it away! Of course, you had to make allowances for celebrities, but it was still the most insulting thing that had ever happened to her. She clearly hadn't made the slightest impression on the great weasel's son.

Even seeing her tremble, Zeke wasn't sorry for telling her the truth. He wasn't clear on what her feelings for Bagley were, but whatever they were, he wanted her to get over them as soon as possible.

"Great tune," he said, tapping a hind paw to the music. "Feel like shaking it up?"

Wendy turned away without another word and went over to her aunt and uncle.

"Didn't expect to see that Whitebelly here," Mr. Blackish remarked. "Glad to see you're holding out for Bagley Brown, Wendy."

This only made her feel worse.

"Are you all right, dear?" Mrs. Blackish said. "You look a little squirrely."

"It's just . . . I don't think Bagley Brown's coming," she said.

"You never know," said Mr. Blackish. "Give him time."

In a minute Zeke ventured over to them.

"Good to see you again, Mr. and Mrs. Blackish," he said. "You don't feel like dancing, Wendy?"

Wendy shook her head. Great-looking as Zeke was, she felt far too miserable and angry to dance. Zeke sighed and walked a few feet away.

Not far off, Mary Lou Silverface was standing with her parents, swaying to the beat. Zeke couldn't help noticing she was giving him the eye. Then, as the birds struck up an irresistible rhythm, every muscle in his body began to twitch. Mary Lou gave him an encouraging smile.

But she wasn't the partner he really wanted, so before asking her, he drifted over to the Blackishes one last time.

"Come on, Wendy," he coaxed. "Just one dance?"

"Well," said Wendy, who'd been watching Mary Lou out of the corner of her eye. "Maybe one."

She let Zeke lead her out onto the needles but refused to smile and tried to dance with as little zest as possible. Before long, however, the most annoying thing happened. Her body started jiggling and vibrating to the bird songs as if it had a life of its own. As other young weasels joined them on the dance floor, she tried to keep a severe look on her face, but after three or four songs, the corners of her mouth turned up in spite of themselves. Even if Zeke didn't have an eye patch or a famous name, he was unquestionably the handsomest weasel and the finest dancer there. She felt proud to be his partner. Best of all, she sensed that he felt proud to be hers.

"I'll show you a great new twirl," he said, grabbing her paw.

The new twirl made her head spin, but it wasn't really an unpleasant feeling. As she whirled round and round, she could tell that other weasels were gathering to watch, but they were all a blur. Everything became such a lovely blur that, even if Bagley Brown had arrived under the pines, she wouldn't have noticed.

THE PATCH

Bagley didn't arrive under the pines. In fact, he wasn't even in the Wainscott woods. He was at the end of the hollow log, keeping watch over the pond.

He'd already been there quite a long time—so long that the half dozen bugs tucked in his cheek were getting soggy. He'd come every day since his tussle with the Whitebellys, and every day the striped fish had accepted his offering from the spiderweb in her usual way. This Sunday seemed the same as other days. It was sunny and warm, the two swans were paddling around, there were plenty of bugs out, the swallows were swooping, a solitary gull was hovering overhead. But the fish weren't feeding. There hadn't been a sign of his striped friend.

Every day now the sun was staying up later. But it finally set, and a dark red stain spread over the pink glow in the west. The swans swam off into some tall green reeds. The lone gull flapped away over Bagley's head, toward the road. Bagley stayed put. He hated traveling after dark but hated even more the idea of leaving without a glimpse of his beloved fish. What if something terrible had happened to her? Human beings were known to fish the pond in rowboats or canoes. What if she was sizzling on one of their grills at this very moment, her lovely green and silver scales turning black?

He heard a deep croak nearby and poked his head out the

end of the log. Off to the left, a half-moon had risen just over the dunes, turning the dune grass silver. To the right, a bullfrog was perched on a rock with his throat all puffed out.

"Hullo," the bullfrog said in a pleasant bass voice. "Fine evening."

"Mm," Bagley said—though he didn't sound as if he meant it.

"Too fine for being all on your own," the bullfrog sympathized.

"True enough."

"No Bridge," the frog said.

"Excuse me?"

"No Bridge."

"There's a bridge over there, I believe—just around the crook in the pond."

"No, no. I meant no Bridget. I use her nickname because, well, I'm kind of fond of her. She's so pretty—for a fish."

Bagley stared. "Is that her name?"

"Bridget. Yes."

"How'd you know?"

"I asked her."

"No, I mean, how'd you know about . . . me?"

"I've seen you here before. What's your name, anyway?"

"Bagley Brown," he said, figuring it wouldn't mean anything to a bullfrog. "And you?"

"My friends call me Paddy," the bullfrog said. "Where you from?"

"The Wainscott woods. By the brook."

"I've been up around there. Nice and buggy, late in the day." The bullfrog cocked his head out at the pond. "Ah. Things seem to be looking up—at least for you."

And there she was, the lovely striped fish—Bridget—making her usual pass in front of the log. The setting of the sun had cooled things off, but a warm gush of relief ran through Bagley. She was safe and sound!

He took a deep breath and spat the bugs out with all his might. The fish plucked at them in her dainty way, then made her usual parting pass, her scales glimmering more beautifully than ever by moonlight.

Bagley bid the frog good night and turned to leave. But a sound in the water made him look back. Bridget had poked her head out of the pond.

"Thank you," she said in a bubbly voice.

"Why—it was nothing," Bagley said, stammering a bit. He was inexperienced at talking to fish—or, for that matter, at talking to someone he'd dreamed about.

"No, it was something," Bridget gently corrected him.

"Only a couple more bugs than usual. For your Sunday dinner."

"Yes, but I wouldn't have had any dinner at all without them. Hi there, Paddy."

"Hiya, Bridge," Paddy said. "Seen any pretty frogs cruising around?"

"To tell you the truth, I wasn't on the lookout." She turned back to Bagley. "I hope this isn't a rude question . . . but are you a marten or a weasel?"

"A weasel."

By wiggling her tail and her underfins at the same time, Bridget could keep her head out of the pond, which let her see the weasel without water distortion. He intrigued her. Terrified as she'd been the first time she saw him—that day early in the spring when he blurted out "Good afternoon"—she'd also been curious, since the greeting seemed to be aimed her way. Why should a beast like that be talking to her? So the next day at the same hour she'd passed the hollow log again. And there the creature was, crouched in the end of it, just as before. She was pretty sure he wasn't a muskrat or a squirrel, and she was also pretty sure that he was staring at her. But he had only one eye to stare with! She'd never encountered a one-eyed animal before. Frogs, eels, perch, turtles, herons: they all had two. Even tadpoles had two. Even crabs—though of course theirs stuck out in the homeliest way imaginable. And while flounders had no eyes on one side, they had two scrunched together on the other.

When she checked the log again the next day, the creature *spat* something at her, and she dove straight to the bottom, horrified and insulted. But peering back up from the depths, she saw that what he'd spat was bugs. They'd landed too far from the end of the log for him to take a swipe at her. The bugs looked plump, too. Most striped bass—this was the sort of fish she was—ate insects only as a last resort, but she'd always had

a weakness for them. In fact, she considered them such a delicacy she sometimes went so far as to throw herself all the way out of the water just to get one. Clearly, if she didn't grab these soon, another fish would, or else some frog. Food was scarce in the pond this year.

She floated up and ate his bugs. They were fresh and juicy, a meal in themselves. After that, she coasted by the log every day at dusk. He was always there, waiting with his luscious insects. She did a bit of research and narrowed him down to a marten or a weasel—though both were said to have two eyes. Word naturally got around about him. And yet, when other fish drifted hopefully by the log, they didn't get any bugs. It was as if he wanted only *her* to have them. Nothing so peculiar had ever happened to her before, and sometimes, suspended near the bottom of the pond in the darkest hour of night, she would wake up for a moment and wonder where the odd creature was, what he thought about.

And tonight, at last, she'd dared to speak to him.

"Why wouldn't you have had any dinner today without my bugs?" he asked.

"Because most of the insects have gone home," she said, surprised that a furry beast could sound so civilized. "Besides, it's getting too dark to see them."

"But earlier."

"Earlier, the osprey was out," Paddy said.

"The osprey?"

"You didn't see him?" said Bridget.

"Was that an osprey?" Bagley said in a hushed voice, re-membering the lone gull hanging over the pond.

His mother had told him about ospreys. They were to fish what hawks were to weasels. They plummeted out of the sky, dove straight into the water, and came up with their catch.

"Chances are, he won't stay around here long," Bridget said.

It was tiring to keep her head up, but after slipping down to fill her gills with water and take a short rest, she poked her head back into the moonlight.

"May I ask you a personal question?" she said.

"Anything you like," said Paddy. "I'm an open book."

"No, I meant—"

"Me?" Bagley said. "Certainly."

"I just wondered," she said. "Weasels have two eyes, don't they?"

"Oh, yes."

"Your other one's behind that patch?"

"Well . . . yes and no."

"Yes and no?"

Bagley hesitated. He never discussed his patch. In fact, he usually avoided so much as thinking about his left eye—though by coincidence the talk of the osprey had just put it into his mind. But somehow he couldn't hedge with the fish. Any interest she showed in him, even if it was only in his patch, was something to be cherished. "Yes, it's where my other eye goes," he told her. "But no, it's not there."

"You mean you lost it?"

"Unfortunately. A childhood accident."

"Oh, dear! A hook?"

"A hook?"

"Fish are always worrying about hooks," Paddy explained.

"Ah," said Bagley. "No, not a hook."

"A beak?" Bridget wondered.

"No, not a beak. Not quite."

"I'm being nosy," she said. "I'm sorry."

"No, not at all! It's just . . . it's just kind of a long story."

"I'd like to hear it."

"Well, it's really more about my father than me," Bagley said, and he smiled wryly, for this was true about everything in his life. "When I was half grown, a terrible hurricane hit Wainscott, and afterwards my father had to reconstruct a tunnel."

"Reconstruct a tunnel," Bridget said. "That sounds important."

"Never knew you weasels liked to dig," Paddy commented.

"We don't," Bagley said. "My father enlisted moles for that. He thumped the ground to guide them from above."

"Is that right?" said the bullfrog. "I'm something of a thumper myself." In demonstration he gave his rock a couple of solid thumps with one of his big webbed feet. Then he let out a fine croak.

"Was it a long tunnel?" Bridget asked as the frog's croak died away.

"Very long," Bagley said.

"How many days did it take?"

"It took nights. They only worked at night."

"Shouldn't have thought it mattered to moles," Paddy commented. "The ones I've met are so blind they don't know day from night anyway."

"It wasn't for their sake, it was for my father's," Bagley explained. "You see, the tunnel's for getting eggs, so it's—"

"Eggs!" Bridget exclaimed, swimming backwards. She happened to have some eggs inside her at that very moment.

"Chicken eggs, not fish eggs," Bagley assured her.

"Oh," she said, and she inched closer again.

"Anyway, the tunnel's under a farmyard, so in daylight it would have been too dangerous."

"Foxes and hawks," Paddy said knowledgeably.

"On top of which, Farmer McGee has a shotgun," Bagley said, "and two tabby cats. But at night they all sleep, so my father could guide the moles."

"But where do *you* fit in?" Bridget said in her sweet, bubbly voice.

"I used to watch him," Bagley said, deeply touched by her interest.

"Your mother didn't mind you staying up late?"

"I'm afraid I sneaked out of the den without her knowing. I'd creep across the farmyard and hide behind a stone or a fence post. Then one night I hid behind a feed bucket someone had left out—this was when the new tunnel was almost to the coop. While I was watching my father, the moon darkened for a second, and I looked up and saw a huge creature falling out of the sky."

"Heading for you?" Bridget said, alarmed.

"Well, for me or my father. Just at that moment my father had his ear pressed to the ground. Between thumps he listened in case the moles encountered a rock. So naturally I jumped out from behind the bucket and warned him."

"And he hid?"

Bagley closed his eye for a moment. "After I called out, he lifted his head and said, 'What on earth are you doing here, son?' Then he heard the wings and looked up."

"And then?" Bridget said breathlessly, so caught up in the story she no longer felt the strain on her fins.

"After that, everything's a bit muddled. I remember my father running over to protect me, and I remember seeing the bird's long talons glinting in the moonlight, and I remember the bird had an enormous head and big yellow eyes. Then it felt as if my left eye was on fire. I screamed and covered my face. When I uncovered it . . ." Bagley had to swallow. "When I uncovered my face, I saw my father climbing into the sky."

"Oh, no," groaned the bullfrog. "Just like my poor old granny."

"The horrid bird got him?" Bridget said.

Bagley gave a brief nod.

"And your eye was just . . . gone?"

Bagley nodded again. The eye was gone—though sometimes it was as if it could still see one thing: his father's body, limp in the dreadful bird's talons.

"It must have hurt worse than a hook in the mouth," Bridget whispered. And though fish are cold-blooded creatures, she shivered.

"I guess," Bagley said. "I think I was in shock for a while."

"You just stayed there?" said Paddy. "What if the nasty bird had come back?"

"I would have been dessert, I suppose. But he didn't."

"Then what did you do?" Bridget asked.

"Well, the next thing I remember is the head mole. Or, I should say, the head mole's head, poking up out of the ground. He wanted to know where Mr. Brown was. They can't see much, but he could tell I was too small to be my father." Bagley gave a somewhat bitter laugh. "The mole wondered if he was 'off getting a bite.' Then he explained that the other moles were tired and hungry but willing to finish, since they were so close to the end. So I thumped them the rest of the way to the coop, then crawled home." He gave a shrug. "Anyway, that's why I wear a patch."

After the weasel stopped talking, neither the fish nor the frog said a word. The only sound was the murmur of the sea. The silent moon had sailed higher, and now another one was suspended like a luminous fish in the depths of the pond.

Fish can't shed tears, but Bridget was feeling a strange sort of prickling in her eyes. It may have come from keeping them exposed to the air too long, but all she could think of was the poor weasel. To lose your father and your eye in one swoop!

It was the bullfrog who finally broke the silence, sending a mournful croak out over the water. "I know a little bit how you feel," he said. "I saw my old granny carried off the same way. Though, of course, I didn't lose an eye in the bargain."

"That's a blessing," Bagley said. "It would be impossible to keep a patch on, going in and out of the water all day."

"True. I'd have to go around with an empty socket." Paddy sighed. "It's hard enough finding a wife as it is."

"What exactly happened to your grandmother?" Bagley asked.

"An osprey got her. Seeing that one today gave me the willies."

"I really don't think he'll stay long, Paddy," Bridget said. "It's so much work, building one of their nests."

"I hate to tell you this, Bridge, but he may have moved into that old one."

"An old nest? Where?"

"On top of the telephone pole, second one up from the beach."

"Oh, dear. Then let's hope we get some rain."

What did rain have to do with anything? Bagley wondered. But before he could ask, Paddy gave a fierce croak. "I wish I could jump high enough to knock that nest off," the frog declared. Then he sat up straight on his rock and said, "Good evening."

A few feet away, a female frog had poked her slick head out of the water.

"Evening," she said.

"Paddy," said the bullfrog, puffing his throat out like a balloon.

"Lily," said the newcomer, looking rather impressed by the display.

"I hope you'll both excuse me," Paddy said, lowering himself into the water. "My skin's getting dry."

"It was nice to meet you," Bagley said.

"Same," said Paddy. Then he said good night to Bridget and coasted off on a moonlit swim with Lily at his side.

Left to themselves, neither the fish nor the weasel spoke for a while. Then Bridget said: "Are you all right? You look a little green around the gills—if you know what I mean."

"I was just thinking of that osprey," Bagley explained.

"Oh, but he shouldn't bother you. They like fish."

Actually, he'd been picturing the bird carrying *her* off. But of course he didn't tell her this.

"I keep thinking about your poor mother," she said. "How did she stand it?"

"She didn't, really."

"Don't tell me you lost her, too!"

"Not right away. But she was never the same after that night."

Bridget dipped underwater for a moment and then came back up and stared at the four-legged, one-eyed creature crouched in the end of the log. Why, she wondered, was she so eager to know his story?

"You managed to get home all right with only one eye?" she asked, hoping she wasn't prying into his privacy too much.

"Eventually," Bagley said.

He remembered staggering back to the den in the death-gray dawn. "There you are, dear," his mother had said, thinking he was his father coming home as usual. "Shall I fix you a snack?" But he'd stumbled straight into his nook of the dark burrow and collapsed facedown in the dirt. Now that he was home, the pain and horror overwhelmed him.

Soon he'd felt a motherly paw on his back.

"Junior?"

He couldn't speak.

"Were you out, Junior? What's going on?"

He turned his head halfway around, good eye up. "A hawk," he managed in a choked voice.

"A hawk? You saw a hawk? When?"

"Just . . . now."

"You *were* out. What on earth were you up to?"

"I was—watching Dad."

"What about a hawk, Junior?" Now his mother's voice was urgent.

"It—it came swooping down."

"But hawks sleep at night."

"A big hawk. With a huge head and huge claws."

After a silence his mother whispered: "An owl."

"An owl?"

"Merciless birds that hunt by night. They're rare on Long Island. Did your father see it?"

Then Bagley let out a heartrending wail. "It took Daddy away," he cried, turning over onto his back. "Into the sky."

As this dreadful scene was flashing through Bagley's mind, he realized the fish had spoken, but so quietly he couldn't make out the words.

"Excuse me?" he said, leaning out over the edge of the log.

"What did your poor mother do when she found out what had happened?" Bridget asked a little louder.

"She fainted. On top of me. I shook her, but she wouldn't wake up."

"Poor you! What did you do then?"

Since she seemed so genuinely interested, he told her the rest of the never-before-told story. After working himself from under his mother's body, he'd tottered out to the brook to get a mouthful of water. But not even a squirt in the face could bring her around. So he made a pillow of leaves for her head and went back to the brook to wash out his eye. By afternoon, when weasels started rolling eggs by to thank his father for completing the new tunnel, he'd fashioned an eye patch out of a piece of discarded snakeskin and a bit of vine. All he could bring himself to tell the visitors was that his father was "gone" and his mother was asleep. It wasn't till late that night that his mother came around. And when she saw his patch and re-membered the owl, her snout turned ashen, and she wouldn't touch the egg yolk he'd separated for her. She lingered on for a few more weeks but never again ventured out of the den, and by winter he was alone.

"You've been by yourself ever since?" Bridget asked.

"Mm."

She listed over to one side to see him better, her big eye catching the moonlight. "I know I've been nosy as an eel," she said. "But will you tell me one more thing?"

"With pleasure."

"It's wonderful of you to bring the bugs every day. But why do you come here? We see muskrats, but never weasels."

Bagley wasn't sure what to say.

"Do you come to look at yourself in the water?" she asked.

"Oh, no."

"Just I heard the swans say the pond makes a lovely mirror. I've always wished I could get out for a while and look in."

"Well, I can tell you, you're absolutely beautiful."

"Why, what a nice thing to say! But if you don't come to look at yourself, why do you come?"

Bagley hesitated, then said: "To look at you."

"Me? Why?"

"Because, ever since I first saw you—it was one day early in the spring when you jumped completely out of the water . . . Ever since then, I've thought about you almost all the time."

"You have?" This was flattering, but it was also perplexing. "Why should a weasel think about a fish?"

"I don't know. I just do."

"But . . . you don't even swim, do you?"

"I could, a little, I suppose. But with my patch and everything, I never do."

She thought how she sometimes wondered about him in the deep of night. And yet, grateful as she was for the bugs, and much as she sympathized about his losing his eye and his parents, the idea of feeling romantic about a creature with feet and fur was ridiculous. Rolling over farther, she took a peek at the moon. "My, it's late," she said, seeing how high it was. "I better say good night. Thank you so much for the bugs and for telling me your story."

"You're very welcome," Bagley said, stung to think of her swimming away.

But she did. Alone, he remained with his head poking out the end of the hollow log, listening to the lapping of the distant waves. There were no more croaks now that the bullfrog had attracted a female. Bagley clenched his sharp teeth, wishing with all his heart for Bridget to return.

And then his wish came true. Her lovely head poked up again.

"You came back!" he said, overjoyed.

"I had to."

"I'm so glad."

"I had to," she repeated. "I just couldn't stand to leave that way."

"How wonderful!"

"I mean, I couldn't stand to think of you thinking about me."

"Why?"

"Because I like you too much."

"But that's fantastic! I like you, too! More than that, I—"

"I mean," she interrupted, "I like you too well to let you think about me. Unless of course you were pulling my fin."

"Pulling your fin?"

"Kidding me—about thinking of me all the time."

"Oh, no! I wouldn't joke about that. If you don't believe me, just come back tomorrow. And the next day, and the next. I'll be right here."

"That's what I mean," she said with a sigh. "I adore your bugs. They're always so fresh—never more than a day old. But if you really feel that way about me, I don't think you ought to come back."

"Not come back? But why?"

"Because it would just cause you pain."

"You mean, you could never . . . think about me?" His voice had become as hollow as the log. "No matter what?"

"I'm sorry. I truly am. But . . . fish are meant for fish." She swam up closer, closer than she'd ever been. "If you weren't so wonderful, I wouldn't have come back just now," she said softly. "But you are. So I couldn't stand to think I was hurting you. You have to promise me you won't come back."

"But I love coming here. I look forward to it all day."

"That's just what I mean! Please promise me. If you don't, I'll be miserable. Wait and see. After a few days away, you won't even remember what I look like. I'm really nothing special, you know. Will you promise?"

She was so close he could have touched her. "If you insist," he said, heartbroken.

"Good. Now go and start forgetting me. It won't take long— that's *my* promise. But, you know, I think I'll always remember you."

She turned and swam off into the depths.

"Good-bye, Bridget," Bagley whispered, staring out bleakly at the silver-plated pond.

SOMETHING

Bagley didn't move for a long time, hoping against hope that Bridget would return once more. But she didn't. So at last he turned from her glimmering home and shuffled out of the log.

Depressed as he felt, his heart started pounding as soon as he came out of the reeds and cattails. As a young weasel he'd been almost reckless about open sky, but since the night of the owl he truly had been "sky-scared," as Zeke put it—particularly after dark.

Before crossing the deserted road, he looked toward the beach and saw, atop the second-to-last of the towering telephone poles, a huge nest silhouetted against the moon. It was on a little platform that human beings must have nailed on top of the pole just so a bird would make his home there. The nest was too far away for him to tell if the osprey was in it or not.

It was late when he got back to his den, so it startled him to hear someone speak as he was about to go inside.

"Bagley boy?"

On the opposite bank of the brook, the moonlight showed up a blaze of white—a weasel's belly. Cuddled against this weasel was another, with radiantly dark fur.

"Evening, Zeke," Bagley said. "Evening, Wendy."

"We've been waiting for you, Bagley boy," Zeke said. "Never knew you were such a night owl."

Bagley winced at the word "owl." But since he wasn't in the moonlight, neither of his visitors noticed.

"Would you like to come in?" he asked politely.

"We better not," Zeke said. "Mr. Blackish had some shooting pains in his tail, so Mrs. B. took him home early—but they're probably getting worried about Wendy by now. We just wanted to stop by and thank you."

"Thank me? For what?"

"For giving me the invite to the Tantails' shindig," Zeke said. "Remember what I said about if there's anything I can ever do for you, just holler? Well, that goes double now."

Bagley had totally forgotten about today's tea dance. "You had a good time?"

"The best," Zeke said, pulling Wendy even closer to him. "We really kicked up our paws, didn't we?"

Wendy looked up from the brook for the first time. "I was pretty mad at you, Bagley," she said.

"I don't blame you," he admitted. "It was rude of me to give away the invitation."

"Yes," Wendy said, looking down again. "It was."

"But you see, Zeke seemed to want it so badly, and I assumed I could go without it, if I wanted to. Then the whole thing slipped right out of my head, idiot that I am. I hope you'll find it in your heart to forgive me, Wendy."

"Well," she said. "Zeke did show me a wonderful time."

"We gave those old fogies a real eyeful, didn't we?" Zeke said proudly. "She's the spiffiest partner you ever saw, Bagley. And only her second time out!"

"I'm glad everything worked out for the best," Bagley said, trying to smile. But it wasn't easy. There was Zeke, with a lovely weasel at his side, while he was in love with a creature who could never love him back, who lived deep in a pond he'd just promised never to visit again.

"See you around, Bagley boy," Zeke said. "Maybe on egg duty."

"Good night, Zeke. Good night, Wendy."

"Good night, Bagley," Wendy said, giving him a crooked smile.

Once the happy pair was gone, Bagley crept into his den and went to bed. In his present mood, sleep would be a blessing. But as soon as he closed his eye, he saw Bridget, her lovely head poking out of the moonlit pond. And he heard her bubbly voice: *After a few days away, you won't even remember what I look like. I'm really nothing special, you know.*

Nothing special! The way she'd come back to ask him not to return—giving up the bugs he brought, just to spare him pain—made her the most special creature he'd known since his father. And then, her last words: *But, you know, I think I'll always remember you.* How wonderful of her to say that! Could she be thinking of him now, saying his name to herself as he was saying hers to himself?

Bagley rolled over on his belly and buried his face in the dirt. It had just hit him—he hadn't introduced himself to her! He'd been so overwhelmed just to be talking to her that he'd forgotten simple manners. He'd told her his deepest secrets, but not his name. Son of the most brilliant weasel who ever lived, and a total dunce!

He hardly slept a wink that night, but in the morning he had more energy than usual. So he headed off to the Double B, hoping egg duty would wear him out. It usually did. Getting the eggs off the straw-covered roosts in the coop without breaking any was always a struggle, and rolling them back down the tunnel was even harder. Though straight as an arrow, thanks to his father's thumping, the second Double B had been dug deeper than the first to prevent another cave-in. The moles weren't used to digging that far down, so the tunnel wasn't level. The downslopes were ideal for egg rolling, but the upslopes made even Zeke Whitebelly pant.

Yet that morning the work didn't tucker Bagley out at all. When he got home, he curled up and shut his eye, eager to escape the torture of thinking about the forbidden pond. But he couldn't. At last, without exactly realizing what he was doing, he got up and headed for the spiderweb.

Bagley was always careful with the web. The worst damage he ever did while pulling out dead bugs was to knock a few jewel-like drops of morning dew off the delicate strands of silk. This morning he pulled out three mosquitoes and two green-tailed flies. It was silly, since he wasn't going to the pond, but he did it out of habit. And once the bugs were stored in his den, he managed to curl up and sleep.

He hadn't brought an egg home that morning—he'd had no appetite—but when he woke up that afternoon, an egg was leaning just inside the doorway. He suspected Zeke of dropping it by. He cracked it open on a stone and sucked up the yolk.

It made him feel peppy. But he refused to let himself go back on his promise and trot off to the pond as usual. Bridget had dragged the promise out of him because she liked him: it was her one gift to him. So he just sat hunched there, staring enviously at the water in the brook, which Bridget might eventually sip. After winding out of the woods, the brook flowed between a potato field and a horse pasture and then ran through a culvert under the road and emptied into the pond.

All of a sudden he went into his den and put the bugs in his mouth as he did every day. But instead of heading for the pond, he just spat the bugs into the brook and watched them float off downstream. He'd promised not to go see Bridget, but that didn't mean he had to quit giving her bugs. Not that the chances were very good of their even reaching the pond. And if they did, she probably wouldn't get any of them. But she just might—and that was something.

LITTLE FISH

This became Bagley's daily ritual. Instead of slipping off to the hollow log, he dropped bugs into the brook. He dropped them in about an hour before late-afternoon fish feeding, to give them time to make their way to the pond. It comforted him a bit.

But, unfortunately, Bridget's prediction didn't come true. A week went by, and then another, but he didn't even *begin* to forget what she looked like. She appeared to him every night in his den, floating in the darkness. As time went by, she became more, not less, clear to him.

Then one night the osprey appeared to him as well. He pictured the bird grabbing Bridget out of the water and carrying her off to his nest atop the telephone pole. He couldn't shake the awful vision out of his mind. If it should really happen, would the osprey's talons kill her instantly? Or would she linger on till the bird dumped her in his nest, her gills still fighting for oxygen as the fierce beak ripped into her flesh? The dreadful possibilities kept Bagley awake all night.

Next morning, he joined the egg squad. But eggs only made him think of nests, and the osprey—and by the time he got back to his den, he knew his promise was doomed. He had to find out if Bridget was all right.

He didn't wait around, for it seemed to him that if he visited the pond now, in the morning, instead of at feeding time, he wouldn't be going back on his word so badly. Of course, he longed to see Bridget with his own eye, but it would be enough just to hear from someone—Paddy the bullfrog, for instance— that she was alive and well.

The pond looked different somehow when he emerged from the reeds and cattails onto the shore. It must be the sun, he decided. Usually it was setting across the water when he came. Now it was just up, at his back, and the tall green reeds that bordered the pond were tinged with gold.

Bagley made his way cautiously through the hollow log and poked his snout out the end. The bullfrog wasn't on his rock. In fact, the only sign of life was the pair of swans, paddling around as usual out in the middle of the pond. Or perhaps not quite as usual. A line of tiny brown shapes was swimming in the wake of one of the majestic white birds: one, two, three of them. Baby swans—cygnets, as they were called.

A bird swooped down over the pond, a large, pale bird with a wide wingspan. The three cygnets immediately climbed onto their nearest parent's back, for protection. It was the osprey.

To Bagley's immense relief, the osprey didn't dive for a fish. Instead, the bird rose up into the blue sky and wheeled sea- ward, sailing across the spit of sand and out over the ocean. The cygnets slid off their downy perch, back into the water. And in a couple of minutes some fish appeared, not far from the end of the log. They were tiny things, hardly more than minnows. But they had stripes.

"Fishies!" Bagley called out.

One of the fish poked his head up. "What are you?" the fish asked in a squeaky voice.

"I'm a weasel."

"What's a weasel?"

"It's a species of carnivorous animal."

"What's carnivorous?"

"Um, that's not really important."

"Where do you live?" the fish squeaked.

"In the Wainscott woods."

"What's that?"

"It's a place not far from here. You've really never heard of Wainscott?"

"Come on. I'm only three days old, what do you expect?"

"Is that so? You speak very well."

"Thank you. Does carnivorous mean you eat fish?"

"*I* certainly don't."

But the little guy still kept his distance. "See you later, Weasel," he said, sinking down out of sight.

"Wait!" Bagley cried.

"Yeah?" the fish said, rising again.

"Do you know a striped fish called Bridget, by any chance?"

The little fish giggled—or gurgled, it was hard to tell which. "Hear that, guys?" he said. "He wants to know if I know Bridget!"

Half a dozen little fish heads poked up, all giggling, or gurgling.

"Who is he?" one of them asked.

"He's a carnivorous species," the first fish said. "He's made of wood."

"I *live* in the *woods*," Bagley said. "Listen, do any of you happen to know if Bridget's all right?"

"She's peachy," said the leader. "Except she says we swim her off her fins. She's our mom, you know."

"Your mom?"

"Yup. Best mom in the pond. If you wait a minute, you're bound to see her. She doesn't like us playing near the surface."

Bagley didn't wait a minute. He said good-bye, turned around, and hustled right out of the log. A mother! He was so crushed that he barged right through the reeds and started across the road without even looking.

This almost got him crushed for good—by the front tire of a bicycle carrying a plump, sunburned human being. He scuttled under the hedge on the other side. But then he slowed to a shuffle. A mother, in just two weeks! She must have already been married the night he spoke to her in the moonlight. No wonder she hadn't wanted him to come back!

He slumped along in such a daze that by the time he heard the growl, it was too late to make a run for it. The cat—a black one with sinister green eyes—was only a few bounds away, streaking across a newly mown lawn. It went through Bagley's mind just to crouch there. Bridget was married—what was the point of going on? But weasels have a powerful instinct for survival. When the cat was almost to the hedge, Bagley dove into a little hole between two roots.

The hole was such a tight fit he had to slither down like a snake. This meant it might well belong to a snake, in which case things would probably take an unpleasant turn. But when he fell into an underground chamber, the shrieks that welcomed him weren't snakish at all.

After a couple of quick blinks, Bagley's eye adjusted to the dark and made out a dozen other eyes around the room: the round yellow eyes of a half dozen panic-stricken chipmunks. One of them gave a squeal and popped up into the chute Bagley had just fallen out of. But in a second the poor fellow came tumbling back down, nearly landing on Bagley, and fled to the farthest corner of the chamber. Bagley glanced up the chute. An evil green eye was peering down.

"Pardon the intrusion," Bagley said. "I didn't mean to barge in."

The chipmunks were too petrified to say a word. Usually weasels ate chipmunks. But meeting Bridget's children had ruined Bagley's appetite.

"Don't worry," he said. "I'll only stay till the cat leaves."

It wasn't a pleasant day for any of them. The cat sat stubbornly by the hole. The chipmunks cowered against the walls of their den. Bagley brooded over Bridget's being a wife and mother.

Weasels are known to attack animals far larger than they

are, and toward the end of the day Bagley lost his patience. But as he was about to shinny up and nip the stupid cat on the snout, a human voice called out in the distance:

"Fatima! Where are you, Fatima? Here, Fat, Fat, Fat! Dinnertime!"

The cat sent two hisses down the hole, then abandoned it. Bagley apologized to his chipmunk hosts, who were all total wrecks, and squeezed up out of their home. The coast was clear. Toward the pond, the sun was sinking. Bagley trotted off in the other direction.

When he got back to his den, it was about the time he usually dropped the bugs in the brook. But he hadn't collected any that morning—and besides, why send presents to a married fish? He ducked into his den and curled up, exhausted. He hadn't slept at all last night, and what with egg-squad duty, meeting Bridget's kids, and escaping the cat, it had been a long day.

But he couldn't drop off even now. After a while, he got frustrated and went out and sat by the brook. His eye settled on the spiderweb. Now was the time of day bugs got stuck in the sticky silk. Some were still alive, since the well-fed spiders didn't always sting them right away, but there were others that weren't struggling anymore.

Bagley walked out onto the fallen limb. Yes, there were four or five dead ones. He pulled out three and dropped them into the brook.

Back in the den, he finally went to sleep.

THE STRAWBERRY MOON

The weather got hotter and hotter, so by June the woods were as dry as Mr. Blackish had forecast. But there weren't any lightning storms to set them on fire. There were no storms at all. One day followed the next without a cloud in the sky.

It was hard on the rabbits. The grasses they liked to munch turned brittle and brown—tasteless, really, and hard on the digestion. But the Wainscott weasels thrived. The brook always provided drinking water, and the McGees' hens kept laying away. At the end of the day, the birds were so relieved to have the heat let up that they sang their hearts out, making the weasels' dancing parties that much livelier.

Zeke and Wendy were the sensation of the season. They danced so wonderfully together that even grand weasels like the Tantails smiled at the sight of them. Mr. Blackish himself softened toward Zeke. He quit calling him Zach.

Wendy had never been so happy in her life. Nothing could have been better than whirling on the pine needles with Zeke. There were only two problems. One, Zeke always led. She enjoyed being led by him—but why shouldn't she have a chance to lead, too? Yet whenever she suggested it, he laughed in the most aggravating way. The other problem was that this was the only thing they ever did together: dance. They hardly talked at all. If she ran into him during the day, he was always with his brothers, and all he would do was wink at her. At dances the music cast a spell over them, and they simply danced. And except for the night her uncle got shooting pains in his tail, he and her aunt always took her home right after every dance. According to her uncle, staying late was nearly as bad as arriving on time.

"Couldn't I stay after you leave just once, Aunt?" Wendy asked at last. "If Zeke had to walk me home, maybe he'd . . ."

"What, dear?"

"Well, *say* something. All we ever do is dance."

"I thought you were wild about dancing."

"I am. But . . . you know."

"Mm," Mrs. Blackish said, smiling. "Well, the First Summer Cotillion's coming up Saturday. It's always the last Saturday in June. Maybe I could get a headache, just after sunset."

Saturday was yet another beautiful day. In the morning a breeze blew off the ocean, but in the afternoon it died down, so Wendy's fur, which she'd fixed several different ways before she was satisfied, hardly got mussed up at all on the way to the pines. Zeke was already there, hanging out with his brothers by the refreshments. As usual, he came straight over and asked her to dance.

They danced and danced, until her feather fell out and she had to dive to rescue it from being trampled. But once again he refused to let her lead. So, much as she loved dancing, she decided to go sit on one of the stump roots. If he complained, she would tell him that Bagley Brown would have been gentlemanly enough to give her a chance.

But just as she broke away, Zeke said: "Look, Wendy girl! They're leaving without you!"

She turned and saw her aunt, with her paw to her brow, being led away by her uncle. And since it was her one chance to stay out on her own, she decided not to spoil it.

After the last dance, the diehard dancers said good night to each other and started going their separate ways. By then a full moon was peering down through the pines.

"I can't believe your aunt and uncle just took off!" Zeke said, leading Wendy toward the stump.

"Maybe Uncle got more shooting pains," she said.

"Wow, that's great!"

"Great? Shooting pains in the tail can be very painful."

"I mean, great that I can walk you to your den. I mean, if that's okay with you."

"Well . . . sure."

"You guys go on home," Zeke called to his brothers, who were cleaning up the last of the refreshments. "I'll catch you later."

So Wendy and Zeke set off by themselves through the moonlit woods. The crickets were making a racket, but that was the only sound.

After a while, Zeke and Wendy both started to talk at once.

"Sorry," Zeke said. "What did you say?"

"Oh, nothing. Just that it's a full moon."

"You know what they call it?"

"What?"

"The full strawberry moon."

"Really?"

"The farmers picked the last strawberries a while ago, but that's because it's been so hot," Zeke said knowledgeably. "Usually they get ripe about now."

"It's a gorgeous moon."

"It is pretty great, isn't it?"

Once they finished with the moon, another silence fell over them. She began to feel frustrated. She had some time alone with Zeke at last, and she was wasting it!

"Look, there's some poison ivy," she said in desperation. "Do you get poison ivy?"

"Nah. Doesn't bother me a bit. You?"

"I'm not sure. I stay away from it."

"Hm. That's smart, I guess."

So much for poison ivy. They walked on in silence, side by side.

There was a clearing near the Blackishes' den. At the edge of it, Zeke stopped beside a fallen tree. The truth was, he'd been wanting some time alone with Wendy, too.

"I was wondering something, Wendy girl," he said, resting an elbow on a shelf mushroom growing out of the tree.

Wendy's heart quickened. "What's that?" she asked.

"Well, I was wondering if maybe we shouldn't get hitched."

"Hitched?"

"You know, married. We're perfect partners, right? I was chewing it over last night, and I couldn't think why we shouldn't get hitched up."

"You couldn't think why we shouldn't get hitched up?"

"Nope, I couldn't. Can you?"

Her eyes flashed. "I most certainly can!" she said indignantly.

Zeke blinked in surprise. "Really? Why?"

"*Why?* For one thing, that's how you ask somebody if they want an egg for lunch, not if they want to get married."

"Oh." He slid his elbow off the mushroom and stood up straight. "Sorry."

"For another thing," she said with a sniff, "I've got to go back to the North Fork in October."

"But you're grown up. You don't have to go back to your folks. Besides, you said you hated those ferryboats. They made you seasick."

This was all true enough. Nevertheless, she turned toward her aunt and uncle's doorway. "That's *not* how weasels propose," she said. "Good *night*."

Zeke leaped after her. "Wendy, wait!"

"What is it?" she said sternly.

Zeke peered left and right to make sure none of his brothers had followed them from the cotillion. Seeing that they truly were alone, he took Wendy's left paw. "I'm sorry, Wendy girl. You know I love you. You're prettier than . . . than . . ." He looked all around, then up. "The moon!"

Wendy looked up, too. It really was about the most beautiful moon she'd ever seen. "No, I'm not," she said, a little less sternly.

"Yes, you are!" Zeke insisted. "You're twice as pretty. Three times!"

"You really think so?"

"Do I!" He squeezed her paw. "You'll think about it?"

"About the moon?"

"No! About marrying me."

"Oh," she said. "Well . . ."

"Well?"

It was impossible not to admire his fine white belly in the moonlight. "I'll tell you what," she said. "I'll think about marrying you if you'll think about letting me lead."

Zeke made a face. So she made one back and turned away. But before she could get far, he grabbed one of her paws and spun her back to him.

"It's a deal," he said—and then, before she could protest, he gave her a kiss, right on the snout.

BEST WEASEL

By July the heat had sunk down even into the Double B, making egg duty harder work than ever. But Zeke and his brothers still volunteered three or four mornings a week. The only weasel who volunteered for more egg duty than they did that summer was Bagley. Bagley rolled eggs every single morning. It helped take his mind off Bridget. In spite of meeting her kids, he just couldn't seem to get her out of his head, or his heart.

When the eggs were rolled up out of the tunnel, at sunrise, a representative of each weasel household would come and collect one or two. When the Whitebellys worked, they often took three, which they richly deserved. One morning, in the middle of July, Zeke told his brothers to roll their eggs home without him.

"Think I'll go along with Bagley," he said, wiping his brow, "and take a dunk in the brook."

In fact, he wanted to speak to Bagley privately. As the two of them trudged off through the dusty woods, he told Bagley he had some remarkable news.

"What's that?" Bagley said, figuring Zeke was finally going to marry Wendy.

"You're not going to believe this, Bagley boy, but . . . Well, Wendy and I are going to get hitched up!"

"Really!" Bagley said, trying to look surprised. "Congratulations."

"Thanks, buddy."

"When's the big day?"

"A week from Saturday. Wedding at three, under the pines, then the reception. The Blackishes are putting it on. We'll be dancing till dawn!"

"Sounds terrific."

"Yeah. Except, I got kind of a problem about my best weasel. If I ask Ben, Bill'll be mad as a hornet. If I ask Bill, Ben'll be mad as a wet hen. And if I ask the twins—you know, like a double best weasel—Bill and Ben'll both have their snouts out of joint. So it hit me. If I ask you, maybe nobody'll get riled. I can just say it's because of how you . . . you know, got us together."

"A week from Saturday," Bagley said. "I'd be honored."

"Great!" Zeke said, slapping him on the back.

Egg rolling was dusty work these days. The slap knocked such a cloud off Bagley's back that Zeke had a little coughing fit.

"You know, I like it hot," he said when he caught his breath. "But I wish it would rain once before the wedding. You get so darn dusty these days, dancing. It comes right up through the pine needles."

"It can't go on like this forever," Bagley predicted. "It's bound to rain before long."

But it didn't. The sunny days continued to march along one

after the next, and the only clouds were the clouds of dust that rose off the dry earth. The Saturday of the wedding arrived without a drop of rain having fallen.

None of the Whitebellys rolled eggs that morning, naturally. However, Bagley did. Once he got home from the Double B, he went through his usual routine of collecting bugs. But while storing the bugs in his den, he realized the wedding created a problem. As best weasel, how could he leave before the end of the reception? And now that the crickets were playing their violins all night, he supposed the weasels really *would* dance till dawn. So he wouldn't be able to drop his bugs at the usual time. If he dropped them before he left for the wedding, they would reach the pond so early that some other creature would snap them up before Bridget even had a chance. It was a silly thing to worry about, of course. She probably never got them anyway. But the hope that she did was the one spark in his life.

Bagley sat thinking on the bank of the brook. Every weasel in Wainscott would be at the wedding, but there might be some other creature who would drop the bugs in for him at the appointed time. Who? Rabbits were silly and skittish—harebrained, really, never remembering anything from one minute to the next. Squirrels weren't reliable either. Half the time they couldn't even remember where they'd hidden their nuts. As for birds, they'd just eat the bugs themselves.

When a shiny green frog's head popped out of the brook, right below where he was sitting, it seemed like fate. Frogs were intelligent creatures. But then he remembered that frogs, too, were partial to bugs.

"Mr. Brown?" the frog said in a familiar deep voice.

"Is that you, Paddy?"

"It sure is. Hope I find you in good health, Mr. Brown."

"I'm okay. But please, call me Bagley. What are you doing way up here?"

"Looking for you."

"Really? Why?"

"Because . . ." The bullfrog paused to clear a frog out of his throat. "Do you remember how I met someone that night in the moonlight?"

"I certainly do. You swam off with her. Lily, if memory serves me."

Paddy smiled. "Well, Lily turned out to be just the frog for me. A few weeks back, we had a batch of tadpoles."

"Congratulations." Bagley smiled back, but as on the night of Zeke and Wendy's visit, it wasn't easy. It was beginning to seem as if he was the only creature on the whole South Fork who wasn't happily mated. "How many kids do you have?"

"Fourteen."

"All healthy, I hope?"

"For the time being. That's what I came about, partly. They're getting bigger every day—and more reckless. Natural, of course. But considering what's happening, we're worried sick."

"What's happening, Paddy?"

"You don't know?"

"I haven't been to the pond since, er, well, only once since the night we met. That was in the morning, and I didn't stay long. What's happening?"

"Well, maybe you better come see for yourself."

"I promised Bridget I wouldn't."

"Oh," the bullfrog said, disappointed. "That's how I was going to get you to help us. I figured you'd want to help Bridge."

"What do you mean?"

"Well, I mentioned you to this old possum I know, and he recognized your name. Said your old dad was about the smartest creature that ever lived. So I figured you might be able to think up some way to help us. We're at our wits' end."

Bagley stood up. "What's wrong?"

"It's the pond. It's—well, you'll see if you come."

"Are you telling me Bridget's in some kind of trouble?"

The frog's big mouth now turned down in a frown. "We all are," he said.

Bagley didn't wait to hear more. He dashed away, his promise and Bridget's children equally forgotten. Of course, he wasn't clever like his father, but if Bridget was in trouble, he would do everything in his power to help her.

At the edge of the woods he checked the sky, then sprinted for the hedge. But just before reaching it, he remembered the green-eyed cat and changed his course for the potato field that lay to the south.

The potato plants were in flower, but even they were dry. Their leaves crackled in the breeze as Bagley scurried along under them. His furrow was particularly choppy, so he hopped over to another, but when he did, frantic squawks erupted all around him. He'd landed right in a covey of snoozing bobwhite quail: father, mother, and six children. The little ones would have been nice and tender—a tasty breakfast—but he let them all flap away.

The potato field ended by the dunes. At the foot of the dunes was a line of shrubs: wild roses, mostly, with some Queen Anne's lace mixed in, both droopy from too much sun. The wild-rose bushes were excellent cover, good and thick, but the thorns made the going so slow and painful that in the end Bagley climbed to the top of the dunes.

The dune grass was only so-so cover, and as he scampered along, bloodcurdling shrieks filled the sky over his head. It was his worst nightmare come true! And there wasn't just one bird diving at him, there were three—four—five—all pale as death. He had nowhere to hide. All he could do was throw himself onto the ground and wait for the claws to pierce his rib cage.

But while the shrieking got louder and louder, Bagley didn't feel any pain. He peered up. The pale birds were still zooming down on him, but at the last second they swerved away. It was always hard to judge the size of things at a distance with only one eye, but now he could see that the birds weren't actually very big. They must, he decided, be terns. His father had once told him about terns, how they build their nests in the dunes and, if you get too close, dive-bomb you to scare you away.

Bagley was only too happy to be scared away. And once he'd put a good distance between himself and the nesting area, the terns called off the aerial attack.

Stopping to catch his breath, he surveyed the beach through the waving dune grass. As far as he could see, there were only three species of animal down there: two kinds of shorebird—sea gulls and sandpipers—and a few human beings. It was too early in the morning for human beings to be lying in the sun. These were standing in the backwash with long fishing poles. They cast their shiny lures out over the waves, reeled in, then cast again.

Bagley continued on, and after a while a nearly empty

parking lot came into view to his right. He climbed off the dunes, skirted the lot, and headed inland along the edge of the road. It was the road he always had to cross to get to the pond. When he came to the place where the hedge ended, he dashed over to the other side and dove in among the reeds and cattails. The stalks rattled as he brushed against them, browner and drier than he'd ever known them. When he came out onto the shore of the pond, he was stunned. The narrow strip of sand was narrow no longer. It stretched out ahead of him for two hundred feet. The hollow log was high and dry. It looked like a big bone bleaching in the sun. The heat had shriveled up the pond to half its former size.

Over the middle of what remained of the poor pond, the osprey was hovering in the breeze. As Bagley watched, the bird dove straight down, smacked into the water with a splash, and vanished. After a second underwater, he resurfaced and flapped awkwardly back into the air, a good-sized fish dangling from his talons.

Bagley's fur crept. The vision that had haunted his nights was real.

THE SWANS

O n his way down the road, Bagley had passed the second-to-last telephone pole. But since he hadn't been thinking of the osprey, he hadn't checked the nest. Now he watched the ruthless bird carry the unlucky fish straight to it.

Once the osprey landed, Bagley couldn't see him anymore. Crouched in the shade of the hollow log, he didn't have a good angle. But it wasn't hard to figure out that the bird was eating his breakfast: fresh fish.

Only now, as he looked from the big nest back to the drying-up pond, did Bagley understand the remark Bridget had made on that silvery night in the spring: *Then let's hope we get some rain.* As long ago as that, she'd been worried about the shrinking of the pond. For when a pond gets smaller, it also gets shallower, and in shallow waters fish are much easier to spot and catch from above. Picking them off would be as easy for the osprey as getting eggs was for the Wainscott weasels. Bagley's eye flicked back to the nest. Could that have been Bridget he'd just seen? Or had the osprey—heaven forbid!—made a meal of her already?

After a while he heard a croak. The bullfrog hopped out of the dry reeds.

"Paddy! That was quick."

"Coming downstream's a breeze," Paddy said. "Quite a change around here, huh?"

"The osprey just caught a big fish and took it back to his nest," Bagley said, his voice shaking a bit. "It may have been Bridget."

"I doubt that. Bridge is pretty smart, you know. There's still one deep place left, and she stays there with her kids. But they've got to feed sometime. And the pond's getting shallower every day."

The bullfrog's opinion of Bridget's intelligence lifted Bagley's spirits a bit. She just *had* to be alive. But still, he couldn't imagine what he could do to help. What was needed was a big rainstorm. Though he'd never been much of a dancer, he knew most of the weasels' dances, and there wasn't a rain dance among them.

"Is there some way to get the ocean to fill up the pond?" he said, thinking aloud.

Paddy shook his head. "When the pond gets full, the human beings dig a cut to drain it out. That's how some of the fish go out to sea. But it doesn't work the other way around. The pond bed's above sea level."

"So it is," Bagley said sadly. "You know, Paddy, there's more shade over here."

The bullfrog was squatting by the rock he used to sit on. "Thanks, Bagley," he said. "But this is fine."

"You don't think I'd hurt you, do you?"

"Well, not really. But a weasel got a second cousin of mine once, and . . . well, instincts are instincts. I've met several charming flies, but it's hard as the dickens for me not to eat them. I hope you're not offended."

"No, I understand." Bagley stared out dismally at the pond again. "I wish I could think of something."

"I know. That osprey's too big and mean to fight. I just thought maybe, since your dad was so brilliant, you might be a chip off the old block."

Bagley sighed, wishing he was—though, of course, if he had

been, he would have fallen in love with a weasel, not a fish.

"I'm afraid the only thing I have in common with my father is our name."

"Hey. Don't feel bad. It was a long shot. I just thought if you checked things out . . . Anyway, it was nice of you to come."

Bagley surveyed the pond once more. He scratched his head. "There's something else different. Other than its being so much smaller."

"The reeds are drying up. It's murder on us frogs. We like to play in the reeds."

"No, something else."

"The nasty smell? It's the algae and everything from the old pond bottom rotting in the sun."

"No, not that." Bagley tried to picture the pond as it had been last time. And then he remembered. "The swans. What's become of the swans? Surely an osprey couldn't eat a swan!"

"No, the swans just left. The place was getting too small for them."

"Where did they go?"

"I heard one of the youngsters bragging about how they were flying to a bigger pond, a couple of miles west of here."

"Hm," Bagley said thoughtfully. He squinted up at the nest on the telephone pole. "Does one fish a day satisfy that osprey?"

"Well, yes and no. It used to. But now that the pickings

are so easy, he eats two or three a day. I think he only eats the parts he likes best and tosses the rest out."

"When does he go out hunting again?"

"Usually around two in the afternoon. He likes a late lunch."

Bagley thought some more and then said: "Listen. I have an idea. But it'll take time." He pointed straight up. "Do you think you could meet me back here when the sun's about there?"

"You really have an idea?" Paddy said, hopping forward.

"Please don't get your hopes up. But it's possible."

"Oh, but that's wonderful! I knew we could count on you!"

In his enthusiasm Paddy jumped right up and offered one of his short front legs to shake. Bagley took it.

"In the meantime you can check on your family, Paddy. And, perhaps, if you have the chance, you could check on Bridget?"

Paddy couldn't speak. What was he doing, shaking hands with a weasel!

"Back here, at midday?" Bagley asked, releasing the frog.

Paddy just nodded. But as the weasel headed for the reeds, the bullfrog found his deep voice.

"Good luck, Bagley Brown!" he croaked.

THE BEACH

agley retraced his steps, crossing the road and then creeping along the sandy shoulder toward the beach. But this time he kept a cautious eye cocked up at the nest.

As he neared the foot of the osprey's telephone pole, he got a whiff of something rotten and glanced into a shallow ditch that ran by the road there. His fur stood on end. There must have been two dozen fish skeletons in the ditch. Many had flesh and scales still hanging on the bones—fish the bird had merely sampled. These were crawling with bugs.

Bagley got away from there as fast as his paws would carry him. He scurried around the edge of the beach parking lot and didn't stop till he was on top of a dune. From there he looked down at the beach. Nothing had changed. There were still only the three kinds of creatures in sight: the sea gulls, the sandpipers, and the fishermen.

As a rule, weasels aren't avid beachgoers. They don't care for sunbathing, and they're not partial to the sorts of shellfish that wash up on the sand. Even the weasels of Wainscott, who live so near the shore and have so much spare time, never go to the beach. And of all the Wainscott weasels, Bagley liked the beach the least. It was more exposed to the open sky than any other place. On hot summer days, colorful umbrellas cropped up on the sand, but they were used by human beings, and except for these, there were no hiding places from birds of prey.

This morning, though, Bagley forced himself to slide down the seaward side of the dune to the beach. Once there, he understood another reason for staying away from it. Bad footing. If a bird dove at him, his paws would spin in the sand.

But he crept on toward the water, keeping a careful watch on the sky. Three gulls were standing between him and the nearest fisherman. He eyed them warily as he drew closer. He'd never heard of a gull killing a weasel. In fact, rumor had it that gulls lived on garbage. On the other hand, he'd never heard of a weasel killing a gull, either. And these gulls certainly weren't small. Their yellow bills looked vicious.

But when he was a few feet from them, he tried hissing and baring his teeth. The gulls looked at him, looked at each other, looked back at him. The largest then opened his impressive wings and took off. The other two followed his lead.

Relieved, Bagley made his way toward the fisherman, who was standing bare-legged in the backwash, surf casting: tossing his line out over the waves, reeling it back in, then casting it out again. His gear was in a pile on the beach behind him. Bagley poked through it. There was a wicker basket, a metal tackle box, a towel, and a tin bucket a lot like the feed bucket he'd hidden behind on the night of his father's death. Disappointed, he headed for the next fisherman, about fifty yards down the beach.

This fisherman was actually a fisherwoman, in a big straw hat. She had about the same gear, except that it included a pair of sunglasses with red frames and a tube of sunscreen. No sign of what Bagley wanted. But as he was about to dash off to the next pile, he heard a hollow splashing sound coming from the bucket.

The bucket was too tall to peer into, and the tin sides were too smooth to climb. "Hello?" he whispered. "Is somebody in there?"

"Who's that?" said a strangled, gurgly voice.

"A weasel," Bagley whispered. "Are you a fish?"

"I *was*," came the gloomy reply. "A young bluefish, to be exact. But now I'm dinner for a human being. Unless . . . I suppose you want to eat me first?"

"No," Bagley said. "I want to help you."

"You're kidding," the fish said.

Bagley put his shoulder to the bucket and pushed with all his might. Nothing happened. It was too heavy.

He checked the fisherwoman. She was still in the backwash, casting her line out over the breakers and reeling it in. He went around to the seaward side of the bucket and tapped it.

"When I count to three, you might throw yourself against this side of the bucket," he suggested.

"Anything you say!" the bluefish replied, sounding a little less gloomy.

Bagley went back around to the other side. "One, two, three," he counted, and then he threw himself against the bucket with all his might.

The fish threw himself against the opposite side at the same instant, and the bucket leaned seaward and then tipped over, sending fish and water splatting out onto the sand. Luckily, the roar of the sea kept the fisherwoman from hearing.

Except for a cut in the corner of his mouth from the hook, the bluefish appeared to be in fine shape. But he didn't make much headway flopping toward the backwash. Bagley approached and, strangely nervous, planted his front paws next to the fish's dorsal fin. It was the first time he'd ever touched

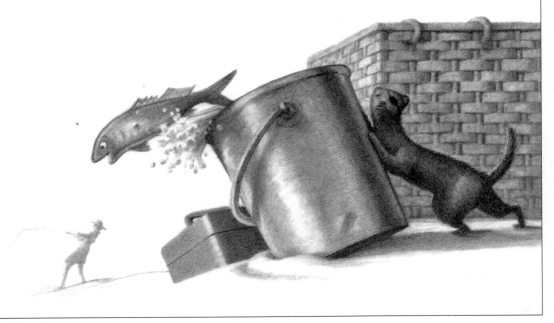

fish scales. They were smooth and pleasantly cool. He gave a shove, then another. Soon the sand became soft and damp under his hind paws.

"You better go back," the bluefish said, gasping. "You're a real lifesaver, Weasel."

"Tell your friends to swim farther out," Bagley advised. "So they won't get tricked by the lures."

"Thanks, I will. And thanks for helping me. Who even knew weasels cared about fish!"

Bagley scurried up the beach just as some backwash swooshed over the damp sand. The bluefish caught the wash and swam out right between the fisherwoman's legs, disappearing into a breaking wave.

Bagley checked the sky. A few gulls were soaring around up there, but no hawks, no owls, no osprey. Continuing down the beach, he encountered a group of sandpipers. But sandpipers are small birds, and they scurried away on their quick little feet at the sight of him.

The next fisherman had a huge belly, hip boots, and a fancy belt with different kinds of lures hooked to it. Like the others, he was busily fishing away; but his gear included a large cooler and a spare fishing rod. Bagley examined the reel on the spare rod with enthusiasm. The fishing line was just what he needed, and there must have been seventy-five yards of it or more wound around the reel. But if he pulled it out, it would get all tangled up. And as for taking the whole rod, it was far too heavy. So he would have to get the reel off.

The line was strong nylon, but weasels' teeth are like razors, and in a matter of seconds Bagley cut the line between the reel and the first eyehole on the rod. Removing the reel from the rod's cork handle was another story, however. It was held on by two steel rings-pushed tightly over the reel's metal flanges. Though strong for their size, weasels aren't large. Bagley tugged at the lower ring with all his strength, then at the upper ring. Neither would budge. His only hope was to loosen one of the rings by gnawing at the cork on the handle. Bagley started gnawing near the bottom ring. The cork was tough. He gnawed till his jaws ached, but still the ring wouldn't give.

He checked the sun. It was climbing higher in the sky. Way down the beach, two human beings with tans almost as dark as weasel fur were carrying surfboards toward the water. In the other direction, there was a family of sunbathers spreading out colorful beach towels.

After a rest, Bagley's jaws still ached, but he started gnawing the cork again anyway. He got so involved in trying to ignore the pain that he forgot to keep a lookout.

When a shadow fell across him, he froze. The rubber toes of a pair of hip boots were two feet away from him. High above loomed the gigantic fisherman. Bending right over Bagley, the man opened the cooler and pulled out a beer and some peanuts. He finished off the nuts, tossed the can aside, and popped open the beer. Then he tilted his head back and guzzled, his Adam's apple bouncing. When he was done, he gave a satisfied belch and crushed the beer can in his hand. He dropped it and headed back to his long fishing rod, stuck in the sand just above the water line.

The crushed can happened to land right on Bagley, but since it was empty the pain was bearable, and Bagley managed to swallow his "Ouch." It was all so unbelievable! His father had told him long ago that human beings tended to be remarkably unobservant, but this took the cake. While digging in the cooler, the fisherman could have reached down and picked Bagley up by the tail. But he hadn't even noticed him!

Bagley started gnawing the cork again—though now only in snatches, stopping every few seconds to check the sky and the fisherman. This technique was easier on his jaw, but it made for slow progress. And with every passing minute the beach was getting more crowded with human beings.

By around noon, when the sun was high in the sky, people began to go swimming. Pausing to look back down the beach, Bagley saw the fisherwoman standing over her tipped-over bucket with a scowl on her face. She collected her gear and left, as did the fisherman beyond her. It was dangerous to cast hooks out in the water when people were swimming.

Bagley gnawed the cork for all he was worth. At last, the ring slipped. The reel slid right off.

But it was heavier than he'd expected. And just then the fat fisherman started toward him, pole over his shoulder. This time, since he wasn't busy gnawing, Bagley noticed how the sand actually quivered with his footsteps.

"Not one nibble the whole last hour," the fisherman muttered. "You'd think somebody warned the darn things off."

Bagley wished he was as far away as the bluefish. But there was still time to make a run for it. This would mean leaving the reel, though, and the reel was his only hope of helping Bridget. If only there was another chipmunk hole to dive into!

That gave him an idea: a hole of his own. He quickly buried the reel in the sand and burrowed down beside it, pulling the peanut can over his head so he could breathe. Then he didn't move a muscle. He just prayed the fat fisherman wouldn't step on him.

"What in the name of Sam?" the fisherman said. "Where's my reel? And how in the world did this rod get all chewed up?"

The big man clumped around for a long time, gathering up his gear and searching for his reel. Once he stepped right on the sand covering Bagley's tail. But again Bagley managed not to cry out. And after five minutes that seemed like five hours, the fisherman stomped away up the beach.

When the sand stopped quivering, Bagley waited another minute and then stuck his head up. The fat fisherman was nowhere to be seen, but less than twenty feet away a pale, skinny man was trying to work the pole of a beach umbrella into the sand. Intent on his progress were his pale wife, two pale boys, and a French poodle.

"Can't you put some muscle into it, Dad?" the older boy complained. "It's boiling out here."

The poodle yapped in agreement. He wasn't clipped and must have been very hot indeed.

"I guess I hit a rock or something," said the father, panting.

"There aren't any rocks on this beach," his wife said testily. "Here, let me do it."

She was considerably bigger than he was, but he shook his head, determined to get the umbrella in on his own. If he succeeded, the poodle would no doubt turn his attention elsewhere, so Bagley set out for the dunes then and there.

The reel must have weighed a pound. After dragging it only two weasel lengths, Bagley had to stop and rest. It would be impossible to get all the way to the dunes without being spotted. He checked the family. The skinny father still hadn't gotten the umbrella in. The younger boy had become bored watching and was playing with a toy truck, rolling it along in the sand.

Of course, Bagley thought. The reel was shaped like the wheels on that truck. He set the reel on its side and started rolling it. Because of the short metal flanges, it didn't roll as smoothly as an egg, but it bumped along.

Soon he was out of range of the poodle's nose. But the sun was now high in the sky, and the farther he got from the water, the hotter the sand became. By the dunes, it started scorching his paws. And though he was in fairly good shape from all the egg rolling he'd done over the summer, he could never get the reel all the way up the mountainous dune. It was too steep, and the sand was too loose.

Fortunately, human beings like to spread their towels near the water's edge, so this part of the beach was deserted. He rolled the reel along the foot of the dunes, using a prancing step that kept his paws from overheating. But he got so wrapped up in keeping his paws unscalded that he forgot to check the sky—till a heart-stopping flutter exploded right over his head.

He squinted up at a huge, blood-red bird with a monstrously long tail, diving right for him. All he had time to do was knock the reel over and burrow under it, hoping against hope that the fierce-looking hawk would hit the metal first and break its beak.

Unlike the terns, the blood-red bird didn't veer away at the last minute. But Bagley felt the impact only as a quake in the sand. He poked his head up, surprised to be still alive. The bloody bird had missed him and the reel by at least ten feet. Odder yet, the bird appeared to be wrecked in the sand.

A boy and a girl raced up to it. "Stupid thing," the girl said, yanking the bird out of the sand. "Think we need a longer tail?"

"I think we need to get out of here," the boy said. "A lousy kite's not worth burning the skin off your feet."

They ran back toward the surf, the red bird under the girl's arm, the long tail hopping along behind them. Bagley unearthed himself and shook the sand from his fur. Now that the danger was past, he realized his paws were burning, too. He turned the reel back on its side and started off again, chanting "Ouch, ouch, ouch" as it bumped along.

After a while he came to a pathway cut through the dunes.

It was invitingly level, so he started rolling the reel down it. Then a boy with a rubber raft came racing toward him, and Bagley had to dive into the dune grass.

The boy ran right by the deserted reel. Bagley crept out of the dune grass and rolled the reel on down the path, once again grateful that human beings were so unobservant.

The path led to a parking lot that was even hotter than the sand. But Bagley didn't mind. He was just glad to be off the beach. What all these human beings saw in it he would never understand.

THE PLAN

When Bagley reached the second telephone pole, he looked up at the big nest. It was impossible to know if the terrible bird was home. Bagley peered into the ditch—the ditch of death, as it should have been called. There seemed to be a new addition: the skeleton of the fish he'd seen in the osprey's claws that morning, only half eaten. Bugs were already crawling on it, but a patch of the poor fish's side still clung to the bones, and there was no stripe on the scales. Please let Bridget be safe in the deep part of the pond, he prayed.

The bullfrog would probably know if she was. Bagley checked the sun. If anything, he was late for their appointment. He hid the reel under some leaves and set off for the hollow log.

Paddy was already there, huddled by his rock. Though he was in the shade, he didn't have his usual wet gleam.

"I kept you waiting," Bagley said. "Sorry."

"That's all right," Paddy said with a dry croak. "How are things going?"

"So far, so good. Did you manage to see your family?"

"They're fine."

"And did you . . ."

"See Bridge? No. I'm sorry."

Bagley's heart sank. "She's not in the deep place?"

"She may well be. I just didn't have a chance to check. You see, my wife got nervous this morning, what with the osprey out. She swam the kids over to the far end and made everybody bury in the mud. It took me forever to find them."

"Well, I'm glad you did," Bagley said, though he wished he had news of Bridget. "You know, the osprey only ate part of the fish he caught this morning. Has he come out for lunch yet?"

"Not yet." Paddy turned and squinted up at the nest. "Soon, probably."

"Okay. I want you to go and tell all the fish to stay in the deep place. No matter what, no matter how hungry they get, they *must* stay there. We need to buy some time. When the osprey goes fishing again, I don't want him to have any luck at all."

"Got you. May I ask what your plan is?"

"It's as much your plan as mine."

"Really? What is it?"

"Remember when you said you wished you could jump high enough to knock that nest off the telephone pole?"

"Uh-huh."

"Well, that's it."

Paddy's eyes always bulged a bit, but now they bulged so much they looked as if they might come out of their sockets. "You think you can climb that pole?"

"I don't know. There *are* a convenient number of spikes sticking out of it, for paw holds. I can try."

"And then you'd knock the nest off?"

"No. I'd lower it."

"Lower it? How?"

"With fishing line."

Paddy blinked. "But why lower it? If you could ever get up there, why not just try and knock it off?"

"I'm afraid it would be a mistake to break it apart."

"Why? I'd like to bust it to bits—in memory of my old granny."

"For one thing, it would be impossible to move if it was broken."

"Move?"

"To the bigger pond where the swans went."

"But why?" Paddy said, astounded.

"If we break it apart here, he'll just use the twigs to reconstruct. But if we move the entire thing, it's possible he'll move, too, and do his fishing over there."

Paddy nodded. This made a certain amount of sense. It took a lot of work to build a new nest, so the osprey would probably go looking for his old one, and no doubt there were more fish in the bigger pond than in this one.

"But the nest's so huge. Even if you could get it down, how could we ever move it?"

Bagley hooded his eye, looking up at the nest. "Some of my fellow weasels might lend a paw."

"You think they would?"

"Well, my father performed quite a service for them. So they might. If I can lower the nest without the osprey seeing, I could run to the woods and try to round up some help. More than likely, they'll be having a dance under the—"

Only then did Bagley remember the wedding. He'd been so busy thinking about Bridget and the osprey, the big event had completely slipped his mind. It had to be two o'clock by now. At three, he was supposed to be best weasel at the ceremony.

"Shoot," he said.

"What's wrong?"

"None of the weasels will be free to help us today. There's a major affair—a wedding under the pines. In fact, I'm supposed to be there."

"You're not going to leave us, are you?"

"Oh, no, they'll get along perfectly well without me. Zeke only chose me as his best weasel to keep his brothers from quarreling about it. I suppose the logical way to proceed would be for you to round up some frogs and toads to help carry the nest to the other pond."

"Well, I could try," Paddy said doubtfully. "But we frogs aren't too great at carrying things, what with our short arms. And toads . . . well, toads are toads. Maybe we better put the plan off till tomorrow."

"And give the osprey another day of fishing? Listen. It's getting later all the time, so I think we better both shake a leg. Don't forget, nobody's to venture from the deep part—nobody. Unless they can bury themselves in the mud." Bagley held out a paw. "Good luck, Paddy."

Paddy hopped right up and shook the offered paw, hardly trembling at all. "Good luck to you, Bagley," he said. "And thanks."

Bagley watched Paddy hop out across the green-tinged sand that used to be the pond bottom. As the bullfrog dove into the water, a flapping in the sky sent a shiver down Bagley's spine, and he lifted his eye just in time to see the osprey rising from his nest, heading out to find his lunch.

THE POLE

Weasels are fairly good climbers. They have strong claws on their paws. But they're no squirrels. And once Bagley got back to the telephone pole, he had serious doubts about his ability to climb it, in spite of the spikes sticking out for repairmen. He'd scrambled up a few tree trunks in his day, but nothing like this. Not that the climb itself frightened him. The thing he didn't want to think about was the osprey returning while he was on the pole, exposed and defenseless.

Anyway, there was no time to waste on second thoughts. He pulled the reel out from under the leaves, leaned it against the foot of the pole, took the end of the fishing line between his teeth, and started shinning up. The pole was an old one, so the wood was rough and splintery, with plenty of places to get a grip. Still, it was hard work. Reaching for the first spike, he gasped for breath, and the line fell out of his mouth.

He had to climb back down to the ground. This time, before starting up, he tied the line securely around his tail, so he would be free to gasp as much as he wanted.

Soon he was clinging to the first spike. He rested there a while, then set out for the second. When he made that, he rested and set out again.

As he was pulling himself up onto the fifth spike, he heard flapping, and a shadow flitted across him. Hot as the sun was, his blood chilled. But squinting up, he saw that it was only a red-winged blackbird, perched on the sixth spike.

"Aren't you a weasel?" the bird asked.

Bagley nodded. Red-winged blackbirds weren't dangerous. In fact, they were usually wary of weasels—though up here on his own turf, the bird had little to worry about.

"I never saw a weasel so high before," the bird remarked.

"Would you be so kind as to tell me something?" Bagley said. "How many spikes are there on this pole?"

"Hm. Eighteen, last time I counted." The bird let out a raucous laugh. "Silly sheep!"

"Sheep?" Bagley said. "Where?"

"There," the bird said, pointing his beak at the telephone wires that stretched between this pole and the next.

Thirty or forty small birds were perched on the wires. "Aren't those sparrows?" Bagley said.

"Sheep," the redwing said scornfully. "One lands on the wire, they all do. One takes off, they all do. Watch!"

He zoomed toward the wire, laughing his head off, and the sparrows all flew away, swarming out over the potato field. It certainly would be helpful to be able to fly, Bagley thought. He looked up. Eighteen spikes. That left thirteen to go. He glanced over his shoulder. The osprey was a few hundred yards away, gliding over the pond. "I sure hope Paddy got the message to the fish," he thought, heading for the sixth spike.

By the time Bagley was halfway up—the ninth spike—he was feeling woozy. He'd gotten far too much sun on the beach and hadn't had anything to drink since leaving the brook at dawn. So the last thing he should have done was look down from such a height. But curiosity got the better of him.

The view swam before his eye, and his paws loosened their grip for an instant—just long enough for him to lose his balance. He was falling from nine spikes up! As he grabbed for

the pole, something stung his left front paw. Then, *oomph*—
something smacked him in the gut.

He was draped over the eighth spike like a sack of feed corn
over Farmer McGee's shoulder. The spike had knocked the

wind out of him completely. But it had also broken his fall.
He hugged it for dear life.

Once he got his breath and his bearings back, he squatted
on the spike and examined his left front paw. A nasty-looking
splinter was stuck through it. As he started to pull it out with
his teeth, he felt faint again and stopped. He grasped the fishing line tied to his tail, pulled up some slack, and wound it

around the spike five times. Then he got the splinter between his teeth again and yanked.

The pain was so excruciating he blacked out. When he came to, he almost passed out again. High above him, where the sky should have been, was the ground. He looked down— and saw down was up. He was upside down, under the eighth spike, dangling by his aching tail.

As he scrambled back up the pole, his left front paw felt very tender. But the splinter was out, and once he was safe on the spike again, he licked the wound till it felt better. Then, without looking down, he unwound the fishing line and headed back up toward the ninth spike.

It was hotter than ever. By the eleventh spike, he had to stop for a rest. The sun was well into the west now: it had to be three o'clock. Under the pines, weasels would be assembled for the wedding, and Zeke would be wondering, "Where's Bagley boy?" Soon Zeke would be naming one of his brothers best weasel in his place.

The osprey flew across the face of the sun, banking high in the air, glaring down hungrily at the pond. Bagley clenched his teeth and kept climbing.

DELAY

he weasels *were* assembled under the pines for the wedding, and Zeke *was* wondering, "Where's Bagley boy?" But even when Bagley was fifteen minutes late, Zeke didn't ask any of his brothers to take over the best-weasel job. In fact, Zeke wasn't all that sorry for the delay. He was a pretty brave weasel, but now that it was so close, this marriage thing scared the fur off him. He was crazy about Wendy, of course, and if he could have seen her, he probably wouldn't have felt uneasy. But on their wedding day weasels aren't supposed to see each other till the ceremony, so Wendy was off on the other side of the crowd, well guarded by her aunt and uncle.

"Maybe old Bagley fell asleep," Zeke said to his brothers. "He's been rolling eggs every morning—and these hot afternoons are great for napping. Maybe you ought to check his den, Benny boy."

"Sure thing, Zeke," Ben said.

As Ben set off, Zeke called after him: "Hey, Ben!"

"Yeah?" said Ben, looking back.

"No rush," Zeke said.

"Oh. Okay."

The news that Bagley Brown hadn't shown up traveled in

whispers from weasel to weasel, soon reaching the Blackishes on the other side of the pines.

"I should have known it was too good to be true," Mr. Blackish grumbled.

"What, Uncle?" Wendy said anxiously.

"Zeke getting Bagley Brown for his best weasel. He probably made the whole thing up."

"Why would Zeke do a thing like that?"

"To impress us, of course."

"But I'm sure Bagley agreed to it," Wendy said.

"So much the worse, then."

"Why, Uncle?"

"Because that means he just plain *forgot*. What could be more insulting than that?"

"But, dear," Mrs. Blackish said, "Bagley Brown's always been eccentric. There's probably another explanation."

"Even so," Mr. Blackish said, scowling. "Making a Blackish wait like this, it's . . . it's just not done."

Wendy did feel a bit flustered. Weasels were sneaking glances at her. But she wasn't really embarrassed. If *Zeke* hadn't shown up, she would have buried herself under the pine needles. But everyone said Zeke was over by the stump. The fact that Bagley wasn't here actually pleased her. Even though Zeke was the weasel for her, she still had a soft spot for the world-famous weasel's son, with his fine speech and his eye patch. She couldn't help thinking that he might have had second thoughts about her, that he might have decided it would be too painful to witness her marriage to another weasel.

"I really am sorry about this," Mr. Blackish said, giving her a squeeze. "But when you get involved with Whitebellys, I guess you have to expect the worst."

"It's all right, Uncle," Wendy said dreamily, picturing Bagley pining away for her in the depths of his den. "A weasel can't have everything, even here in Wainscott."

THE NEST

Bagley, of course, was far from the depths of his den. In fact, he was higher up than he'd ever been in his life. He was just pulling himself onto the fifteenth spike of the telephone pole.

He'd always figured the air grew fresher the higher you went, but when he pulled himself up onto the sixteenth spike, he got a whiff of something truly disgusting. By the next spike the smell was even worse. Did it have something to do with the telephone wires? he wondered. At last he reached the eighteenth spike, the topmost one, and from there it was an easy hop to the crossbar. At each end of the crossbar was a brown ceramic knob that held a wire in place. He sniffed his way out toward one of the knobs. It wasn't the wires.

Once he climbed onto the platform, he realized the stink was coming from the huge nest. And when he chinned himself up on the rim of the nest and looked in, he gagged. The nest was a big bowl of bones and rotting fish heads.

He tried to shut out of his mind the thought that any of those heads might be Bridget's. She just *had* to be safe at the bottom of the pond. He also tried to shut thoughts of his own safety out of his mind, though he knew perfectly well that if the osprey returned to find him clinging to the nest, his choice would be simple: stay put and be ripped to shreds or throw himself off and splat on the ground like a broken egg.

Holding his breath, Bagley heaved himself into the nest. It was made of interwoven sticks and cattails and cornstalks, some quite big around. He undid the fishing line from his tail. As he threaded it around one of the sticks, the line slipped out of his paw.

He dove for it and landed right on a rotting fish head. A milky fish eye stared straight into his. How could anybody stand to live in such a dump? But he'd caught the line. If he hadn't, it would have fallen all the way to the ground, and the long climb would have been for nothing.

This time he was more careful. After checking on the osprey, he pulled up some extra line and coiled it in the nest. He threaded the end around a sturdy-looking stalk and pulled the slack through. Then he threaded the end around a twig on the opposite side of the nest—going from six o'clock to twelve o'clock. Next he went to nine o'clock, then to three o'clock. Finally he tied it all off in the center.

He climbed out of the smelly nest and gulped down some fresh air. Then he slipped a paw around the line that was hanging out and walked to one end of the crossbar. He looped the line around the ceramic knob and, using the knob as a cleat, tugged on the line with all his might. The nest didn't budge. It was just too heavy.

To lighten it, he climbed back in and started heaving the bones and fish heads over the side into the ditch below. As before, he breathed as little as possible and dwelled as little as possible on the chance that one of the heads might be Bridget's. Still, it was the worst job he'd had since guiding the moles right after the owl killed his father.

As he tossed out the last hunk of rotting fish, a chorus of chirruping cheers rose up nearby. Bagley looked around and saw a dozen sparrows perched on the opposite rim of the big nest.

"Wonderful weasel!" chirped one of the little birds.

Bagley wiped a paw across his brow. "Kind of you to say," he said, smiling uncertainly. "But why am I wonderful?"

"These are our favorite perching wires," the sparrow told

him. "We adore the fresh sea breeze. But that osprey stinks everything up."

"Filthy bird," chirped another sparrow.

"Greedy glutton," chirped a third.

"We'd help you clean up, if we could," said the first. "But we're too small. And frankly, we're scared of weasels."

"I understand," Bagley said. "But how would you like to help get rid of the nest entirely?"

"Get rid of it entirely? How?"

"Well, maybe you could round up some of your friends and help me push it off."

"We'd like to—but I don't think we'd want to get that close to you. No offense."

"Hm. Well, somebody has to hold the line, I suppose."

As Bagley climbed back down onto the crossbar, the sparrows flew off. Soon they returned with three dozen of their friends and crowded onto the platform.

Bagley grabbed the line with one paw and pointed toward the next pole with the other. "Push it over that way," he called up. "We don't want it falling onto the crossbar."

"Got you!" said the head sparrow. "Okay, guys, heave ho!"

The birds all put their small shoulders to the nest and pushed, chirruping like mad. The nest moved an inch.

"Heave ho!" the leader cried again.

More wild chirrups. The nest moved another inch.

"Heave ho!"

Another inch. And then another.

At last the nest was tottering on the edge of the platform. Bagley looped the line an extra time around the knob and said: "Okay, everybody, one more push!"

The cheer the sparrows gave when the nest slid off was so shrill that Bagley was glad the osprey was cruising over the far side of the pond just then. The nest fell only a few feet before the line tautened and stopped it.

The big nest swayed under the crossbar, suspended by the cradle of line Bagley had made. Using the knob as a cleat again, he easily lowered it another six inches.

The birds all flew out onto the wires. "Why not just let it

crash down and break into a jillion pieces?" asked the head sparrow.

"He'd just use them to build a new one," Bagley said. "I want to move it to another pond—get rid of him for good."

The sparrows all nodded in unison. "Wonderful one-eyed weasel!" they cried.

"But what about you?" asked the nearest bird. "How will you get down?"

"Same way I got up," Bagley said, holding the line tightly. "I'll climb."

"Well, good luck," the sparrow said doubtfully.

Bagley wound the line a few times around the knob so the nest wouldn't slip unless he released the pressure. Then he looped the line over a shoulder and climbed down to the top-most spike. From there he tried going down headfirst. The sight of the ground far below made him dizzy again. He turned around and tried climbing backwards, tail first. This was no good either. He felt clumsy and couldn't see where the next spike was.

He climbed back up and crouched on the crossbar, at a loss.

"Poor weasel!" cried the head sparrow. "If the osprey comes back and finds *you* up here instead of his nest, he'll peck your eye out. I wish I could lend you my wings."

"Same here," Bagley muttered.

But as he looked from the birds on the wire to the nest suspended a few feet below him, he had an inspiration. He unwound the line till it was looped only twice around the

knob. Then, holding the line loosely in his paw, he jumped.

He landed in the nest. One of his back paws slipped between the interwoven sticks, but the nest held. He was safe, and he still had the line. Feeding it out little by little, he began lowering the nest, with him in it, slowly to the ground.

"Resourceful weasel!" cried the sparrows. "Hurray!"

It was exhilarating, letting himself down little by little, with the sparrows cheering overhead. For the first time in his life, he felt as if he'd accomplished something remarkable. Nothing like the Double B, of course—but still quite a feat. When he was about halfway down, he checked the pond. The osprey was still circling over it. Paddy must have gotten the message to the fish to stay in the deep part.

Bagley was pretty proud of himself. Everything was working out as he'd planned. But bumping to the ground knocked

the pride out of him quickly enough. There was no welcoming party of frogs and toads. The nest was down in one piece, but unless it was moved to the other pond, all the work and risk would have been in vain.

Bagley climbed out of the nest and sat on a stone by the side of the road, licking his tender paw. Should he go to the hollow log? But if he left the nest here, and the osprey returned, the bird would just start flying it back up to the platform, twig by twig. Somehow it had to be hidden.

Not far away, at the end of the ditch of death, there was a wild-rose bush. That would make excellent cover. But when Bagley got up and tried to shove the nest that way, it wouldn't budge. He sat back down on the stone to think. Would the sparrows help again?

Just then, he heard a raucous laugh. The redwing was buzzing the telephone wire. All the sparrows took off. They flew farther and farther away, till they looked like a puff of smoke on the horizon.

"Silly sheep!" the redwing cackled.

Bagley shook his head sadly as the jokester winged off across the potato field. It didn't seem like a time for joking. Somehow he just had to get help to move the nest. Where was that bullfrog?

"Paddy?"

His throat was so dry he had to clear it and try again.

"Paddy!" he called, louder. "Where are you, Froggie?"

FROG'S LEGS

Hot and parched as he was, Bagley would have been really envious if he could have seen his frog friend at that moment, for Paddy was sitting in the deliciously cool brook, deep in the shade of the Wainscott woods. But Paddy wasn't feeling particularly blessed himself. His hind legs had never been so worn out in all their days. It was hard work hopping upstream—and he'd done an awful lot of swimming before starting up the brook.

After leaving Bagley by the hollow log, Paddy had hopped across the dried-up pond bottom. It was a dangerous stretch. Any number of birds considered frogs a treat. But he'd made it to the water.

Just before ducking under the surface, he looked back and saw the osprey leaving its nest. He submerged and did the frog kick for all he was worth, heading for the middle of the pond. Soon he ran into a pair of perch. Perch were reliable fish who understood the pond sign language, so Paddy told them to spread the word that fish should spend the afternoon in the deep place at any cost. Unfortunately, he didn't know sign language for "Bridget." He'd never gotten the hang of the bubbly underwater speech fish use either, and with the osprey prowling the sky, going to the surface to talk wasn't a good idea at all.

The perch split up to spread the word, and Paddy swam straight for the far crook of the pond. He would have liked to search for Bridget, but he was too worried about his family. And when he got to the muddy place near the bridge, his wife, Lily, wasn't buried. She was hopping back and forth on the bank, beside herself. Twelve of the kids were safely under the mud, but the two biggest tadpoles had gone off somewhere.

"And now the osprey's out hunting again," Lily said, wringing her small hands.

"Don't worry, dear," Paddy comforted her. "He won't pick on Tod or Tad—they're too small." But he wasn't really sure of this, since all the fish were going to be hiding in the depths.

Lily wasn't convinced either. "How could they do this?" she wailed.

"Any ideas where they might have gone?"

"I don't know, Paddy. They were watching those human beings before."

"What human beings?"

"On the bridge."

Paddy looked around at the little white bridge. There were seven men standing on it. Five of them had deep brown faces, two were pinkish. Buckets and bushel baskets and long-handled nets were scattered around at their feet, and the men were tossing things into the water on strings.

"Crabbers," Paddy said. "They're using chicken parts as bait on those brainless crabs. I'll bet you anything Tad and Tod are over there sneaking nibbles."

Paddy swam straight over to the bridge. The water beneath it was murky but shallow, and as he'd guessed, there was a congregation of hungry crabs on the bottom. Crabs really were the stupidest creatures. Any fool could see the strings tied around the chicken feet and chicken wings. But the crabs went for them anyway, following the bait as it was pulled up close to the surface, mindlessly clawing away at the food. Then a net would swoop down into the water and scoop the silly things up.

And there, sure enough, were Tod and Tad. When a crab didn't see the bait, Tod and Tad nibbled away at it, following it all the way to the surface. If a net came down, they just slipped through the holes.

Paddy was rather amused. It was a pretty smart way to get a meal. But he rounded the kids up, and once they were back on the muddy bank, he gave them a lecture on the dangers of ospreys and of not obeying their mother.

Once all fourteen tadpoles were safely buried in the mud, Paddy told Lily he had to leave again.

"Not with that osprey out," she declared.

"Sorry, sweetie. I have to."

"Says who?"

"I promised Bagley."

"Who's Bagley?"

"The one-eyed weasel I was talking to the night we met. Remember?"

"Sort of," said Lily, who'd noticed very little that night besides Paddy's impressively puffed-out throat.

"I promised to round up some frogs and toads," Paddy went on. "To help Bagley move the osprey's nest to the next pond."

Paddy considered his wife's mouth the prettiest and widest in the whole pond. It now dropped open so far he could see almost to the base of her lovely long tongue.

When she closed it, she felt his sloping forehead. "You're not well," she said. "You need a good long rest."

"I'm fine."

"A mud bath will do you good."

"But I *have* to go."

"What on earth are you talking about? In the first place, that nest is on top of a telephone pole. How do you expect to get it down?"

Paddy looked at his webbed feet. "Well, I'm not sure," he admitted. "Bagley's taking care of that."

"A little old weasel's going to get that nest down? You've been getting too much sun, Paddy. And even if he *did* get it down, where do think you're going to find enough frogs and toads to move it? No frog with a brain in his head is going to leave the pond with that osprey out and about. And as for toads, you won't even be able to find any. Toads! Huh!"

Paddy continued to contemplate his feet. She was absolutely right. But much as he would have liked a nice long mud bath, he felt he owed it to Bagley at least to try. And besides, even if there was only a slim chance of success, it was worth the attempt. Getting rid of the osprey would improve life for everyone.

He gave a deep croak. "I've got to go," he said.

Lily knew by the croak that he meant it. "Well, then," she said, "I'm coming with you."

He looked up, smiling a lopsided smile. "I appreciate that, sweetheart. But what if the kids come up and find you're not here? They'd panic. They'd start splashing around, and before you know it—"

"Okay," she said with a shudder. "But you be careful, Paddy. And not just of the osprey. I wouldn't trust any weasels, either, even if they do have only one eye."

Paddy gave her a kiss. "I'll be careful," he promised.

He *was* careful, too, hugging the bottom as he swam around the edge of the shrunken pond. But every twenty strokes or so,

he surfaced to get a breath and check on the osprey's where-
abouts. Usually the fearsome bird was off over another part
of the pond, but one time Paddy poked his head up just in
time to see a whitish blur streaking toward him out of the sky.
He dove straight for the bottom and wriggled under a stone
on the pond floor just as an explosion went off overhead. In
an instant, lethal talons closed around the stone. The bird
pulled up the stone instead of the frog. When he flapped back
into the air and saw what he had, he dropped his catch with
an angry squawk. The stone fell back into the pond and came
to rest on the bottom only a short way from the quivering
bullfrog.

Not even this close call convinced Paddy to give up trying
to recruit help. But it was just as Lily predicted. The few frogs
he encountered refused to leave the water, and he never even
saw a toad.

Discouraged, he swam to the neck of the pond nearest the
hollow log and gingerly stuck his head out. The osprey wasn't
far off but was looking in the other direction, flying north.
Paddy waited till the beastly bird was over the bridge, then
made a dash for the reeds.

The sprint left him gasping. And once he reached the roadside, four cars in a row went by, kicking up so much dust he
nearly choked. But when the dust settled, he saw an aston-
ishing sight. Things were flying out of the nest up on the telephone pole. He crossed the road and hopped toward the pole.
The things flying out of the nest were bits of bone and fish.

He couldn't see who was doing the tossing, but he detected fishing line dangling down the pole to a fishing reel on the ground. Up above, a congregation of sparrows was perched on the side of the nest, watching whoever was inside.

Paddy would have bet his hind legs it was Bagley. But when he opened his mouth to call up, he couldn't produce a single croak. His throat was too dry from the dust. All he could do was squat there and watch in admiration.

After a while the sparrows flew off, and in a moment, sure enough, Bagley scrambled out of the nest. The remarkable weasel climbed right out to the end of the crossbar. The sparrows returned with dozens of their friends and began pushing the nest off the platform. As it was about to topple, Paddy jumped backwards, afraid it might land on him. But it didn't fall. It ended up swaying underneath the crossbar, held up by some miraculous means. It was just as Bagley had planned by the hollow log. He was actually going to lower the nest in one piece.

This was all Paddy had to see. He bounced off down the roadside, away from the beach. If a weasel could risk his life getting that nest down—not for himself but for the benefit of the pond dwellers—he could certainly keep his end of the bargain and round up some help for moving it. Since frogs and toads were no good, he would have to try to round up some of Bagley's weasel friends.

When he came to the brook, he jumped in and took a good swig to wash the dust out of his throat. Then, for the second time that day, he set out for the Wainscott woods.

It was upstream all the way, which was why his hind legs were so worn out when he got there. Luckily, underneath a fallen limb with a spiderweb on it, the water swirled like a whirlpool bath. It relaxed his muscles wonderfully—and nothing could have been more pleasant than staring up at the luscious selection of bugs on display in the web. But unluckily there was no time for enjoying it. He had to get a move on.

The instant he reached the top of the bank, somebody grabbed him by the neck.

"Hah! A bullfrog!"

"Ow!" Paddy croaked, peering around at a weasel. "Please, don't kill me!"

"But this is great!" the weasel proclaimed. "Even better than finding a best weasel. Zeke's crazy about frog's legs!"

THE GOOD SAMARITAN

Paddy!" Bagley called out. "Where are you, Paddy?"
Bagley was still sitting on the stone by the foot of
the telephone pole. He kept calling and calling, but
there was no answer. He was beginning to think he
would have to find someone other than the bullfrog to help
him. Yet the redwing had scared off all the sparrows, and there
weren't any other creatures in sight.

But he had to get the nest at least under the wild-rose
bush before the osprey's return. "Anyone?" he cried. "I really
could use some help!"

"Well," said a voice, "I suppose I'm someone."

It came from startlingly nearby. Bagley looked all around
but saw no one. "May I ask who said that?"

"Me," came the reply.

Bagley looked down. There weren't even any bugs or
worms around. It was too hot. "Excuse me," he said, "but
who? Could you possibly move so I could locate you?"

"You're sure you want me to?" the voice drawled.

"If you wouldn't mind."

"Well, okay."

Bagley jumped off his seat. The stone had moved! He
watched a head and clawed feet slip out from underneath it.

"Why, you're a turtle," he said.

The turtle blinked in the sunlight.

"I don't think I ever sat on a turtle before," Bagley confessed.

"I never had a weasel sit on me," the turtle replied. "You must be awfully tired."

"I'm exhausted, to tell you the truth."

"This heat's very sapping."

Bagley agreed. "I wonder, are you feeling too sapped to help me move this nest under that bush?" he asked.

The turtle contemplated the nest. Then he contemplated the bush. "You'd rather live in the shade," he concluded.

"No, it isn't my nest. Weasels don't live in nests. It's a matter of wanting to hide it."

The turtle nodded understandingly. "Hiding is a wonderful thing, isn't it? I do it all the time."

"You'll help me, then?"

"I don't see why not. I'm not quick, but I've been told I'm fairly powerful."

"Thank you! My father always said turtles are good samaritans, and now I see it's true."

The fishing line was still hooked over the crossbar of the telephone pole. Bagley yanked some slack down and tied a loop in it—a yoke, which the turtle put his head through. Bagley went behind the nest and pushed, but his efforts didn't contribute much. The turtle pulled the nest along pretty much on his own, slowly but surely.

"You're a savior, Turtle," Bagley said when the nest was

under the thorny bush. "Do you care for flies, by any chance?"

"Mm. Love them."

"I'd be honored if you'd drop by my den sometime. It's by the brook in the Wainscott woods. There's a big spiderweb there. I'll get you the juiciest flies available."

"I'll make a point of it. How's the road?"

Bagley crawled out from under the bush and looked both ways. "All clear, after the blue station wagon."

A blue station wagon whizzed by, and once the dust settled, the turtle started across. It was torture to watch him, he moved so slowly. And when he was only a little over halfway, a dirty white convertible came racing out of the beach parking lot and up the road, its tires spinning on the sandy pavement. Bagley tried to give a warning, but his throat was so dry that nothing came out but a rasping sound. He shut his eye, unable to watch the helpful turtle get squished.

Tires squealed. Cracking his eye open, Bagley saw an astounding sight. Not all human beings, it seemed, were completely unobservant. The convertible had stopped to let the turtle cross.

DRY AS DUST

When the turtle was safely into the reeds and rushes on the other side, the convertible sped away, and Bagley set back to work. He gnawed through the fishing line just above the yoke. Then he crept back to the foot of the telephone pole and started yanking the fishing line down from the crossbar. After a while the line fell on top of him in a big coil. He climbed out from under it, rolled the reel under the wild-rose bush, wound the line in, and hefted the reel into the nest.

By this time he was feeling pretty peculiar. A dried-out rose petal, pink with brown edges, was caught on a thorn on one of the lowest branches of the bush, a couple of inches over his head. But when he reached up to touch it, he missed. It was really farther away. And when he blinked to clear his blurry vision, fireworks went off in his head. His eyeball felt as if it was drying up.

He had to get something to drink. That was his problem: he was all dried up. He crept out from under the bush and tried to estimate how far it was to the brook. But as he was about to stumble off in that direction, a shadow danced across the road. His eye jerked up. And for a second or two his vision was absolutely clear. The osprey was flying in from the west, an eel dangling from his claws.

Bagley dove back under the wild-rose bush. There was some flapping overhead, then the eel splatted onto the ground. Or, rather, *two* eels. Bagley blinked, more colors exploding in his head. What it was, was two halves of one eel. The osprey had bitten it in two and the halves had fallen. They writhed in the dust for a moment, then were still. While Bagley stared at them in dismay, a terrible ruckus erupted up above.

"Where's my nest? Where's my nest?" Who ever knew ospreys had such piercing voices? "There's hardly a bit of wind!" the bird screamed. "What happened to my nest?"

Needless to say, no one answered him. Bagley held his breath. Then, more flapping. It grew louder. The osprey landed on the ground, only a few hops from the wild-rose bush.

Luckily, his back was to it. The bird jabbed viciously at one of the eel halves and gobbled it up. Then he grabbed the other in his beak, tilted back his head, and let the thing slide down his gullet. But this meal didn't seem to satisfy him. He let out a fur-raising squawk and screamed:

"I want my nest!"

Just as he started looking around, a motorbike came puttering up the roadside, carrying a young man with no shirt on. With another squawk, the huge bird took a couple of clumsy steps and flapped awkwardly into the sky.

Bagley huddled by the nest, unable to see where the osprey had flown. Once the motorbike passed by, he peeked out from under the bush. The fearful bird wasn't on the telephone pole.

As far as his blurry vision could make out, the bird wasn't on any of the telephone poles.

Bagley had no choice but to start off along the side of the road. His breathing had become quick and shallow; if he didn't drink something immediately, he would die. After a few steps he came to the ditch of death, fuller than ever of rotting fish parts, thanks to all the bones and heads he'd tossed out of the nest. But it didn't stink anymore—at least, not to him. His nostrils were dried up, and he could no longer smell things. He tottered along the edge of the ditch, nearly falling in.

A ways up ahead a fuzzy greenish curtain stretched off to the east. It was the hedge, his old route between the woods and the pond. The sight of it heartened him, and for a few steps he scooted along at his usual under-the-open-sky clip. Then a car went by. He had to stop, choking on the dust cloud.

As the dust settled over him, so did a strange numbness. He wiped a paw feebly across his face but couldn't feel anything, didn't even realize he'd knocked his patch up and exposed his empty socket. Blinking his eye only made weird colors swim like tadpoles across darkness, like Paddy's kids in the deepest part of the pond . . .

Bagley keeled over. He lay there on the shoulder of the road, unable to move. He couldn't see anything—even the strange colors had drained away into blackness. But he could still hear. He heard a crow cawing somewhere far away. He heard a car horn honking, probably in the beach parking lot. He heard the dry rustle of the breeze in the hedge.

Then he heard a sound that stirred the darkest depths of his memory: the whoosh of great wings descending. The osprey had spotted him. For an instant, as he realized he was about to meet the same end as his father, he felt pure terror. But then the terror faded into simple sadness. The second Double B had been finished, but he hadn't managed to move the nest to the other pond. He would die a failure, not having helped Bridget in the least.

UNDER THE PINES

It was only a few minutes before this that the other weasel had collared Paddy on the bank of the brook.

"Frog's legs!" the weasel cried, his paws digging deeper and deeper into the poor bullfrog's neck. "The perfect wedding present for Zeke!"

"Zeke?" Paddy sputtered, choking. He'd heard Bagley mention that name: the weasel who was getting married.

"Yeah," the weasel said. "My big brother."

"Who are you?"

"Bill Whitebelly. What's it to you?"

"It's just, I'm—agh."

"You're what?"

"I'm—agh—I'm choking."

"Course you're choking. I'm strangling you."

"But I'm—agh."

"What?"

"I'm a friend of—agh."

"A friend of what?"

"Ba-a-a-agh."

"Bag?"

"Ba-a-agley."

"Bagley? Bagley Brown?"

Paddy nodded as best he could with the weasel throttling him. And the weasel actually loosened his grip a bit.

"This *is* Bagley's place," the weasel said thoughtfully. "You're really a friend of his?"

"Good friend."

"Then tell me this. Where is he? He's holding up the whole works. Zeke sent Ben first, but Benny couldn't find him—so I said *I* could. He's supposed to be best weasel, you know." A cloud passed over Bill's face. "Though why Zeke picked him instead of me I'll never figure." Then the cloud cleared. "But here I find a frog instead. Funny how things work out sometimes, huh?"

Paddy nodded, realizing that all weasels weren't equal in intelligence. This one had two eyes but seemed almost dim. "You know Bagley Brown?" he asked.

"Know him! It was just a couple of months ago I gave him a good licking." Bill puffed his chest out, figuring a bullfrog would never know it had been the other way around.

"He needs help," Paddy said.

"So what?"

Paddy sighed. This was basically the same response he'd gotten from the frogs when he'd swum around the pond.

"Let's go," Bill said, dragging the bullfrog away by the neck.

"You're going to kill me?" Paddy croaked.

"Nah. I'll give Zeke the honors. It's his big day."

Poor Paddy was dragged across dirt, over twigs, through

dusty fallen leaves, then onto pine needles that pierced his delicate skin. But the needles themselves weren't half as gruesome as the mob gathered on them. It was solid weasels, dozens of them, all with sharp-looking teeth. As they completely surrounded him, he quivered from his green head to his webbed feet, too scared to speak.

"A little wedding present for you, Zeke," Bill said proudly.

"Frog's legs!" exclaimed the one he was talking to—the biggest of the bunch. "Yum!"

"Want to finish him off? Or should I?"

"He's all yours, Billy boy," Zeke said generously.

Billy bared his razor teeth. But before he could sink them into Paddy's throat, Zeke said, "Not now—or he won't be fresh. We haven't even had the ceremony yet. You couldn't find Bagley?"

Bill shook his head. Then he laughed. "Funny thing. This frog says he knows him. Says Bagley needs our help."

"What?" cried a new voice. A female weasel with shiny, close-set eyes and a pretty blue feather behind one ear broke through the crowd.

"Wendy girl!" Zeke exclaimed. "We're not supposed to see each other."

The female weasel's snout turned pink. "Oh, dear, I forgot. I saw Bill dragging this frog, and I was so curious . . ."

"Well, it's okay by me," said Zeke, who was actually glad to see her.

"Did you say you know Bagley?" she asked the frog.

Paddy was still too frightened to make a sound. But he managed to nod his trembling head.

"Where is he?" Wendy asked.

Paddy wheezed down a couple of breaths. "He's—he's—he's getting the nest down off the telephone pole."

"What nest?" she asked gently. "What telephone pole?"

"Osprey nest. Pole near the pond."

"And he needs help?"

Paddy nodded vigorously.

"You hear that, Zeke? Remember what you told him?"

"What's that?"

"You said if he ever needed anything—*anything* . . ."

Zeke was staring at Paddy. "You mean that's what you're doing in the woods, Frog? You came from Bagley?"

Paddy nodded again. Zeke turned on his brother. "And you wanted to eat him?" he snapped, cuffing Bill across the ear. "Lord, you're as dumb as a rabbit!"

Poor Bill. He wobbled dizzily away, the same as when Bagley cuffed him, and walked straight into the stump.

"Can you take us there, Frog?" Zeke asked.

"Well, I'm pretty dead—er, tired," Paddy said, rubbing his sore neck. "Why don't you go on ahead, and I'll meet you. You know the road near the pond?"

Zeke shook his head. "Never been over that way."

"I know it!" Wendy cried. "I know the way!"

"It's the second telephone pole from the beach," Paddy said. "I'll go by the brook and meet you there in a few minutes."

"Thanks, Frog," Zeke said. "And sorry about the frog's legs stuff. Didn't know you were a pal of Bagley's."

Paddy smiled wanly and headed toward the brook, not at all sorry for a break from the weasels. As the frog hopped away, Zeke climbed up onto the stump to make an announcement.

"Listen up, everybody," he said. "The wedding's off for the moment. Bagley Brown needs our help."

The magical name Bagley Brown rippled through the crowd. Even grand weasels like the Tantails and the Blackishes agreed that if Bagley Brown needed help, they would gladly give it.

"Let's go!" everybody cried.

"You okay, Billy boy?" Zeke asked, jumping down off the stump.

"I guess so," Bill muttered.

"Okay, then. Lead the way, Wendy girl!"

THE LEADER

Some brides might have been annoyed at having the groom climb up on a stump at the last minute and announce that the wedding was off. And truth be told, it wasn't one of the things Wendy had been daydreaming about for the last couple of weeks. But she didn't really mind. Since the night of the strawberry moon, Zeke had let her lead twice, out on the dance floor, yet both times had been a little disappointing—partly because he'd stepped on her paws, but mostly because he'd worn such a sour expression. But now she had her true chance.

It was marvelous, bounding through the woods with the entire community of weasels in her wake. Rabbits and squirrels fell over themselves to get out of their way, and a snake who was sunning himself in the clearing where Zeke had proposed to her slithered swiftly into his hole.

When they broke out of the woods, the sun was up ahead, sinking a bit in the west, blinding after the shade of the trees. Wendy didn't so much as break stride. She didn't bother checking the sky for hawks, either. She headed straight for the end of the hedge. Her eyes adjusted to the brightness just before she got across the open patch—just in time to see a full-grown red fox step out from under the hedge.

She put on the brakes. All the weasels put on the brakes. The fox had his ears pricked, and he showed his teeth.

For a second Wendy felt faint. But then, strangely enough, she felt the opposite of faint—incredibly wide awake, wider awake than she'd ever been in her life. Instead of shrinking behind Zeke and the others, she did a wonderful thing. She showed *her* teeth back. Not only this, she let out a warning hiss. And after a couple of seconds all the weasels behind her took the cue and did the same thing.

It was a bewildering moment for the fox. He loved weasel. Weasel wasn't easy to come by, for weasels were quick as the devil. And now a whole feast of them had delivered themselves up to him. It was like a dream.

And yet it was a case of too much of a good thing. The biggest of them wasn't a quarter his size, but there were so many, all showing their pointy teeth. What's more, the way they were hissing, he could tell that if he grabbed one, the others would nip him. It galled him to give up such a gourmet meal, but somehow it didn't seem worth the risk of having his shiny red coat ripped by all those needlelike teeth. So he

gave a shrug and trotted off toward the potato field to look for quail.

For a while none of the weasels twitched a muscle or said a word. But when the fox was a good distance away, Zeke jumped up to Wendy's side.

"Way to go, Wendy girl!" he cried, clapping her on the back, almost as if she was one of his brothers.

In fact, his brothers had remained at the rear of the pack when they met the fox. But now Ben sauntered up to the front.

"Foxes," he said scornfully. "You see the fleas on that guy?"

"Yeah," said one of the twins, following Ben to the front. "He had a whole circus on him."

"I'll say," the other twin chimed in. "They're worse than rabbits. They must be about the mangiest critters in the whole—"

"Come on!" Wendy said impatiently. "We're wasting time!"

She dove ahead under the hedge, not even bothering to

look over her shoulder to see if the others were following. They were. Zeke kept right on her heels, and all the rest streamed after the two of them. A chipmunk who'd just come out of a hole between some roots of the hedge took one look at the cavalry charge of weasels and dove back in headfirst. A black cat with green eyes caught sight of them from the back porch of a summer house but decided against giving chase. They were moving too fast, and it was just too hot.

At the end of the hedge, Wendy put on the brakes again— not because of another fox, but to check the lay of the land. There was the road Bagley had crossed so carefully the day he'd taken her to the hollow log. To the right, the road wound inland. To the left, it led toward the dunes and the beach. She counted to the second-to-last telephone pole.

"It looks just like all the others," she said. "Except that platform on top."

"Farmer McGee probably put that up there," said Mr. Blackish, panting a little. "The platforms encourage ospreys to nest on them, and ospreys keep away chicken hawks."

"I wonder what Bagley's up to there," Wendy said. "Think we ought to wait here for the bullfrog or go straight over?"

"It's kind of open here," Mr. Blackish said, scanning the sky. "There might be a hawk or— Wendy, look!"

Wendy looked where he pointed. A hawk was diving out of the sky, heading almost directly toward them. It was different from the hawks on the North Fork, though. It had a whiter breast and a wider wingspan.

"Over there!" Zeke cried, pointing. "A dead weasel."

Now Wendy looked where Zeke's paw was aimed. On the roadside, only a few yards away, a weasel was lying on its side. Unlike Zeke, she recognized the weasel immediately—for she'd once had a bit of a crush on him.

"It's Bagley!" she cried.

Without pausing to consider if he was dead or not, she raced toward him. Zeke stayed right behind her, and behind him came Mr. Blackish and all the other weasels. Having just practiced on the fox, not one of them hesitated. As soon as they'd surrounded Bagley, they looked up and hissed at the diving bird, all of them baring their teeth.

The osprey was every bit as startled as the fox. But for him the decision was easier. He rarely tried for prey on the ground, anyway—he wasn't made for it. He'd just been so angry and frustrated at finding his nest stolen that he'd wanted to take it out on someone, and he'd seen this silly weasel stagger and fall over on the roadside. But a skinny lump of fur and bones certainly wasn't worth risking his gorgeous plumage to all those nasty-looking teeth. A half second above the ground he swerved sharply toward the beach, glided down the road, then wheeled back over the shrunken pond.

As soon as the vicious-looking bird was gone, a car with two surfboards on top came thundering out of the beach parking lot, heading right for the weasels.

"Come on, let's get him out of here, quick!" Wendy cried.

The Whitebelly brothers hoisted Bagley up and carried him into the shade of the hedge just as the surfers went by in a cloud of dust. Once the body was set down, several weasels cried out in alarm. Every one of them stared.

"Holy red hen!" Mr. Blackish said in a hushed voice. "It *isn't* an affectation."

For Bagley's snakeskin patch was still flipped up, exposing his empty eye socket.

"Yikes," Zeke said, clapping a paw over his own left eye.

"Ouch!" cried Bill, doing the same.

But Wendy just leaned over the body and gently put the patch back in place. Then she felt Bagley's brow.

"Dead?" the twins asked.

"I'm not sure," Wendy said. "But look at his lips. He's dry as a bone."

"I believe the brook is just over there," said Mr. Blackish. "It doesn't look as if there's much hope, but we should at least try."

The Whitebelly brothers lifted the limp weasel again and, with the others all crowded around, carried him along the side of the road. Soon the brook came into view, winding off to the right between a potato field and a pasture with chestnut horses grazing in it. The weasels set Bagley down on the edge of the brook, and Wendy scooped some clear, fresh spring water into his mouth. His mouth didn't move, but she made sure the water went down his throat.

When Bagley coughed and spat, she cried:

"He's alive!"

Bagley's eye half opened. It was lusterless and blank. And though his lips moved slightly, no sound came out.

Wendy scooped up more water. "Drink," she said, holding her paws to his mouth.

Bagley drank. He drank several pawfuls. Then his eyelid closed, and he passed out again.

"Let's take him back to the woods," Zeke suggested.

"Good idea," Mr. Blackish said, his eyes shifting nervously from side to side. "It's too open for comfort around here."

"Where you going, Wendy?" Zeke said.

Not far from where they were gathered, the brook ran into a dim culvert under the road. Wendy had heard a "Psst" from inside it.

"I just need to get out of the sun a minute," she said over her shoulder.

The culvert was a gigantic pipe of rippled metal. Once she was into the shade of it, she whispered, "Did somebody call me?"

"I did, miss," said Paddy, who'd arrived there a minute before the weasels came over with Bagley.

Wendy's eyes adjusted quickly to the shadowy place. "Why are you hiding in here, Frog?" she asked.

"Well . . ." The truth was, Paddy wasn't anxious to socialize with all those weasels again. But this one had been kind to him. "Is Bagley okay?" he whispered.

"He was dry as a bone, but we hope maybe he'll come around. We're going to take him back to the woods."

"Ah," Paddy sighed.

"You don't think we should?"

"No, no, go ahead. It's just I'm afraid he'll be disappointed."

"Disappointed? Why?"

"Because his plan didn't get carried through."

"What plan?"

A car passed by overhead, making the whole culvert shiver.

"What plan?" Wendy repeated when things quieted down.

"Do you have a minute?" Paddy asked, looking out nervously at the other weasels. "It's kind of a long story."

"Sure," Wendy said.

BY THE BROOK

Bagley opened his eye and saw he'd gone to heaven. It was a dreamy place. It smelled clean and fresh, not dry and dusty, and felt soft as a cloud. There were little white blossoms scattered around, and a necklace of diamonds hung in the air, shimmering in the celestial light.

"Bagley boy? You awake?"

Bagley turned his head slightly. The angel's voice bore a strange resemblance to Zeke Whitebelly's.

"You're back! About time!"

Bagley lifted his head, blinking at the angel's grinning face. "Oh, no," he said, seeing it *was* Zeke. "How did you die, Zeke?"

"What are you talking about, die? There's nobody dead around here—except some of those bugs over there."

Bagley sat up. He was in a nest of leaves on the bank of the brook outside his den. The necklace of heavenly diamonds was the spiderweb. A shaft of slanting light was hitting the dewdrops on it, making them sparkle. But stuck in the strands were the dead bugs Zeke was talking about. It didn't make sense that there could be dead bugs in heaven.

"Not dead," Bagley mumbled, half to himself. "It's morning. I've been—I've been asleep since . . . Gosh, I really slept!"

"You can say that again!" Zeke said.

Memories jostled into Bagley's groggy brain. He remembered the shrunken pond. He remembered gnawing the cork fishing rod on the beach, rolling the reel in the hot sand, scaling the telephone pole with the line tied to his tail, lowering the nest with the help of the sparrows, pulling it under the wildrose bush with the help of the turtle, watching the osprey devour the poor eel. But what had happened after that? He'd been parched—that much he was sure of. He'd started off in search of the brook, and he'd keeled over. And then there'd been the whoosh of great wings descending on him.

He swallowed. How odd that he should be alive! And another odd thing: he wasn't thirsty now. Looking away from Zeke, he saw a nutshell full of water by his leafy bed.

"How . . ." He swallowed again. "How'd I get here, Zeke?"

"We found you by the road. You were dry as a stick, old buddy. But you're going to be A-one in no time."

"Wasn't . . . wasn't a big bird coming down to get me?"

"I'll say! Biggest old bird you ever saw! But he skedaddled when he got a load of us."

"Us?"

"All of us. We were all there—every weasel in Wainscott. The wedding, you know."

Bagley blinked a few times, trying to piece this together. "How did you know to come look for me?" he asked.

"Well, it was like this. You were supposed to be my best weasel, right? But you didn't show, so I sent Ben out to look for you. When he comes up empty, Bill jumps up and says *he'll* find you. You know what those guys are like. But he doesn't find you either. He finds a frog instead. Right here, as a matter of fact."

"Paddy?"

"Didn't get his name. A bullfrog—nice, juicy one."

Bagley gulped. "You didn't—"

"Nah, don't worry. We *almost* ate him. But then he said he was a pal of yours."

"And he told you about the nest?"

"Well, that mostly came out later. When he was talking to Wendy, in that tunnel thing."

"Wendy?"

"Yeah. That frog took a real shine to her." Zeke laughed, giving Bagley a nudge. "Can't blame him, can you?"

Bagley nodded, smiling. "I guess I should congratulate you on your marriage."

"Not yet, Bagley boy. We aren't hitched yet."

"You're not?"

"How could we get hitched without a best weasel?"

"Oh, dear. I owe you an apology. I got completely tied up with the nest."

"That's okay. Except it's been a pain in the tail, not being hitched. The Blackishes won't let me hang out here on the night shift. Wendy's been taking nights, you know. I got days."

"Nights? Days?" Bagley sat up. "But you found me yesterday, didn't you?"

"Yesterday! Are you kidding? You've been out a week."

"A week!"

"Uh-huh. For a while there, it was touch and go. But this spring water did wonders—that and a few egg yolks. You'll be back in commission before you know it."

A whole week, gone! Bagley tried to think back, to grab at some part of that missing week. All he could remember was a beautiful fish, shimmering in and out of his dreams.

He jumped up.

"Easy, boy," Zeke said, grabbing him. "You're going to be A-okay, but you got to take it slow."

Bagley did feel dizzy. "But what about the nest?" he asked. "Did the osprey get Bridget?"

"Don't know any Bridget. But that nest—zowie! And I always thought egg rolling was fun!"

"What do you mean?"

"I mean, that nest was a blast."

"But . . . start at the beginning, could you?"

"The beginning? Well, I guess it started when Wendy girl went into that tunnel thing under the road."

"The culvert?"

"Whatever you call it. That's where she talked to that old frog. Or I guess the frog did most of the talking—told her all about you and the nest. Listen, you just relax, Bagley boy, and I'll give you the lowdown."

So Bagley lay back in the leafy bed again and listened to Zeke's story.

THE LOWDOWN

By the time Wendy walked out of the culvert and rejoined her friends by Bagley's limp body, she was a weasel with a mission. She'd listened to the frog's story, and Paddy had managed to convince her that it was important to Bagley, as well as to all the creatures who lived in the pond, to move the nest to a larger pond that lay to the west.

But before worrying about moving the nest, the weasels moved Bagley back to his den in the woods. There they divided themselves into two groups. The older weasels nursed Bagley, the younger ones formed a search party to look for the nest.

The search party set out at moonrise. Once they got back to the beach road, it didn't take them long to find the nest under the wild-rose bush. They were all staggered at the size of it. None of them could figure out how Bagley had ever gotten it down from the top of the pole. But with dozens of paws, it was easy enough to carry, and there was plenty of moonlight to see by.

They carried it down the road to the deserted parking lot and along a path through the dunes. Once they were on the beach, Wendy acted as advance scout, marching ahead of the rest, keeping a sharp eye on the night sky. But the osprey must have been off sleeping somewhere after his long day of hunting, for they never saw so much as one of his tail feathers. The only creatures they encountered were a few sleepy gulls and some noisy human beings around a bonfire.

"The gulls took off, but those human beings—they didn't even notice us go by," Zeke said. "I swear, if they weren't such big monsters, they wouldn't last ten minutes."

After a couple of miles, the beach turned into a spit of sand between the ocean and another pond. This pond was far bigger than the first one, and there were some swans floating in it, bluish white in the moonlight, their sleeping heads tucked under their wings. By then the weasels were sleepy themselves, and most of them naturally wanted to dump the nest and go home. But Wendy wouldn't let them. She insisted they put it somewhere high up, where the osprey would use it.

"What a kick that was, Bagley boy!" Zeke reminisced. "But there's something we couldn't figure. There was a reel in the nest. Where'd it come from?"

"From a fisherman, down on the beach," Bagley told him.

"That right? He just gave it to you?"

"Well, not exactly. But anyway—you found a telephone pole and pulled the nest up?"

"Nah. None of the telephone poles around there had one of those platforms on top. But we found a dead pine with a spiffy crook in the branches."

Bagley could just picture it: the nest riding along on the backs of all the weasels, the big pond with the sleeping swans,

the dead pine in the moonlight. He wished he'd been there himself. "Who climbed up with the line?" he asked.

"My brothers and me. What a gas! Course, I wanted to do it on my own. But Wendy put her paw down. 'You're a married weasel now, Zeke,' she says. 'Or almost.' Pretty funny, huh?—me, almost married! But anyhow, we got the line up. Though by then it was almost sunup."

"It must have been a heck of a job."

"It was. But I got to admit, that tree was a piece of cake compared to a phone pole. How you climbed that pole in the hot sun I'll never know."

"I was lucky," Bagley said. He was sitting up again, fascinated. "So you got the line up. What happened then?"

"Then we pulled up some slack and tossed it down on the other side of a limb. You'd already done the hard part, making that web thing for the nest. The others just tied it on. Then they hooked the other end of the line around a root and started pulling. It took a while, but they finally got it up. Me and the boys fixed it in place. Then we climbed back down and high-tailed it out of there, all of us. By the time we got back here, it was too late for getting any eggs, so we took naps and went out mouse hunting. Boy. You forget how much work it is, hunting mice!"

"But what about the osprey? Did he move to the other pond?"

Zeke shrugged. "You got me. That pine was dead, though—

there weren't any needles on it. So if he flew over that way, he'd be bound to spot the nest."

Bagley bit his lip, worried.

"We did the right thing, didn't we?" Zeke asked.

"Oh, definitely! I'm sorry—I ought to be thanking you. It was fantastic of you all to do so much for me."

Zeke grinned. "Never had so much fun in my life."

"And thanks for taking care of me, too. It must have been incredibly dull, sitting around here all day."

"Well, it wouldn't have been so bad, out here. But you do go kind of stir-crazy, stuck in the den."

"I was so bad off I couldn't lie outside?"

"Nah. It was raining so hard. Six days and six nights, non-stop. Today's the first day I could bring you out."

Surveying the woods again, Bagley could tell that it had rained. *That* was why the air smelled so heavenly, so sweet and fresh. The blossoms he'd noticed were wildflowers that had sprung up by the brook. Green shoots had sprouted, too, and nothing looked dusty anymore. Come to think of it, he could even detect a change in the spiderweb. It was a different shape than it used to be. The rain must have been fierce enough to knock the old one down, forcing the spiders to rebuild.

"But that's wonderful!" he cried.

"Well, the rabbits are tickled pink," Zeke said with a shrug. "But it's been so wet we haven't had a single dance."

Bagley was thinking about the level of the pond. But he

nodded sympathetically. "It looks as if it's going to be beautiful today," he said. "I imagine you could have a dance this afternoon."

"This afternoon?" Zeke squinted up at a small strip of sky visible through the canopy of leaves. It seemed to him the slender patch of blue was shaped just like Wendy. "Not a bad idea," he said, perking up.

"Why don't you make it a wedding?"

"What!"

"Well, why not? I'm feeling better by the minute. That is, if you still want me for best weasel."

"Want you! Listen, Bagley boy. I'm really glad you came around, because there's something I've been wanting to get off my chest."

"That yolk stain?"

Zeke peered down at a smear of yellow on his fur and quickly licked it off. "Nah, something else," he said. "It's just, back in the old days, I used to think you kind of put on airs. I mean, with the eye patch and everything."

"That's understandable," Bagley said. "It probably does seem a bit ostentatious."

Zeke pushed his cap back and scratched his head, unsure what "ostentatious" meant. "I mean, weasels said you wore it in mourning for your dad or something," he went on. "But I figured it was like . . ." He looked down and kicked at a piece of moss. ". . . like me doing a back flip out on the needles. You know? I never thought you'd really lost an eye."

Bagley sat up, frowning. "Did somebody look under the patch while I was unconscious?"

"Oh, no! It was just kind of flipped up when we found you."

Bagley winced at the thought that he'd made an exhibition of himself. "Unfortunate," he murmured.

"But it's a good thing," Zeke protested.

"That I lost my eye?"

"No, I mean, it's good for weasels to know. How'd you lose it, anyhow?"

"Carelessness, basically. But that's all water under the spiderweb." Bagley smiled. "Glad you don't mind a one-eyed best weasel."

"Mind! Are you kidding?"

Hearing pawsteps, they looked around and saw Zeke's brothers. They were coming from the Double B, rolling three eggs: Ben and Bill an egg apiece, the twins sharing one.

"Hey, boys!" Zeke called out. "Look who's back among the living."

After parking their eggs, Ben and Bill and the twins encircled Bagley's nestlike bed. They clapped him on the back and congratulated him warmly on not dying.

"This calls for a celebration," Ben declared.

"Yeah!" Bill agreed. "Let's eat!"

The twins nodded enthusiastically and started cracking eggs. During the feast, Bagley got to hear the tale of taking the nest to the big pond all over again, this time with several colorful

additions about the individual exploits of the Whitebelly brothers. In the old days, Zeke would have bragged the loudest, but now he just smiled and let his brothers talk. Something—Wendy, perhaps—had changed him a bit.

Only when the feast was over did Zeke bring up the wedding scheme.

"Today!" Ben exclaimed.

"That's Bagley's idea," Zeke said. "Think you could spread the word, boys?"

"Could we!" Bill cried. "You bet."

"But don't go by the Blackishes'," Zeke warned them.

"Why not?" asked the twins.

"Because Wendy'll be asleep. She sat up all night with Bagley. What would be great is if we could get everybody together under the pines. Then I'll drop by the Blackishes', real casual, and ask her and her aunt and uncle to come out for a walk. Then we'll just show up, and the whole thing'll be a big surprise."

"Great!" Ben said, picking a glob of egg white off his snout. "That'll knock 'em right on their tails!"

"If we've got to spread the word, we better get a move on," said Bill. "We ought to get cleaned up, too."

"Why don't you go home and fix yourself up, Zeke?" Bagley suggested. "I'll be fine."

"No way. Wendy said not to leave you, no matter what."

But Bagley was anxious to slip off to the pond to find out about Bridget. If he couldn't locate her, maybe he could find Paddy.

"I'm fine, honestly," he said.

"You sure?"

"Positive."

"Well . . ."

"I'll be under the pines at three. This time I promise."

"Okay, then."

"And thank you for everything."

"No sweat."

"Thanks for the eggs, guys."

"Sure thing, Bagley!" the other four said. "We'll get rid of these shells for you."

So the five Whitebelly brothers took off together, carting away the eggshells. As soon as they were out of sight, Bagley got up to go. But then he heard his name from the brook and saw a shiny green head poking out of the bubbly water.

"Paddy! I was just thinking about you."

The bullfrog hopped up onto the bank. "I've been thinking about you, too. I wanted to come sooner, but all that rain stirred the pond up so much I couldn't find the mouth of the brook till today."

"Well, your timing's perfect. I just woke up about an hour ago."

"So I saw."

"You've been here a while?"

"Since just after daybreak."

"But why didn't you say anything?"

Paddy looked around warily. "Tell you the truth, weasels still make me nervous. Especially those ones with the white bellies. That big one called me juicy."

"His bark's worse than his bite," Bagley said. "How's the pond? Is it full?"

"Almost. It's wonderful!"

"And the osprey?"

"Gone."

"Gone? You're sure?"

"Absolutely. He hung around a while the day after you . . . the day after I talked to that nice girl weasel in the culvert. But he left in the afternoon, and we haven't seen him since. Then yesterday our swans came back. They said he's living over by that other pond now."

Bagley clapped his paws. "It worked!"

"It sure did. Now the kids can go out and play without our skins turning gray with worry. They're becoming frogs, you know. Losing their tails and getting legs. Fantastic thing to behold." Paddy's wide mouth formed a huge smile. "We all owe you more than we could ever say, Bagley."

But Bagley didn't even hear the last remark. He was staring off at the bejeweled spiderweb. "And what about . . ." He took a deep breath. "What about Bridget? Have you seen her?"

"Sure," Paddy said. "Saw Bridge just yesterday. She's looking great. Nice and plump. Everybody in the pond's been eating like crazy, you know, now you got rid of that nasty old bird for us."

"Thank goodness," Bagley said, lifting his eye.

There was a narrow strip of blue visible through the leaves. It seemed to him that it was shaped just like a fish.

WIFE AND HUSBAND

At around two-thirty Paddy headed back downstream for the pond, and not long after that Bagley headed for the pines. A huge crowd of weasels was assembled there, talking in hushed, secretive voices. But at the sight of Bagley they all crowded around him, bombarding him with questions. Some wanted to know how in the world he'd lost his eye long ago; others, how in the world he'd gotten the nest off the telephone pole last week. About his eye he didn't say much, only that he'd had an unfortunate childhood accident, but he went into a bit more detail about the nest, explaining how he'd had help from the sparrows and the turtle. Nonetheless, they insisted on a spike-by-spike account of his climb up the pole.

"But that would be so dull," he said. "It was just one spike, then the next. Anyone could have done it."

This didn't satisfy them at all. But their clamoring for information was interrupted by Bill Whitebelly rushing up to announce in an important voice that Zeke and the Blackishes were heading their way. The weasels scattered, hiding behind the trunks of the pines.

Before long, Zeke and the three Blackishes strolled onto the needles, Zeke and Mr. Blackish discussing the change in the weather. When they were almost to the stump, the weasels all jumped out from behind the trees and broke into the chorus from the weasel wedding song.

The three Blackishes didn't look quite as overjoyed by the surprise as Zeke had expected. In fact, their faces all fell. Zeke had forgotten to take into account that they might have liked to groom themselves for the occasion. Still, while Mr. Blackish grumbled about Whitebellys, Mrs. Blackish just ducked behind the stump to fix her fur, and Wendy was soon won over by the triumphant look in Zeke's eyes. He'd intended it as a wonderful surprise—so she decided to take it that way.

As she smiled around at all the weasels, she noticed Bagley. "Bagley!" she cried. "You're up!"

He gave her a bow. "Thanks in large part to you, I understand."

"Oh, no. I just sat by your bed."

"All night long, when you should have been sleeping. And from what I've heard, there was a lot more."

"Moving the nest, you mean? That was nothing compared to getting it down off that pole. And there were dozens of us."

"My dear weasel!" Mr. Blackish exclaimed, stepping forward. "So glad to see you up on your paws again!"

"Thank you, Mr. Blackish."

"You're here to . . ."

"To stand as best weasel to Zeke."

"Ah!" Now Mr. Blackish was all smiles. "How splendid! In that case, what are we waiting for?"

"Everybody move back from the stump, please!" cried the twins, acting as ushers. "It's time for the wedding!"

Weasels don't go in for elaborate weddings. The bride has a bridesweasel—Mrs. Blackish, in this case—and the groom has a best weasel; but the ceremony is brief. The couple simply declare their love for each other and then kiss, sealing the bond.

But there was yet another delay in store for this wedding. It didn't take the twins long to clear the area around the stump of everyone but Bagley and the Blackishes and the wedding couple. And Wendy made her declaration in a clear, sweet voice. But then a silence fell over the proceedings.

Wendy kept her eyes fixed on the pine needles, but all other eyes were concentrated on poor Zeke. He'd completely lost his voice. When he opened his mouth, not a sound came out.

Wendy hadn't minded Bagley's being late for the last wedding, but Zeke's failure to return her declaration of love made her snout burn with mortification. She sneaked a look up at him. His mouth opened, but still nothing came out. Weasels began to whisper.

When Bagley felt the strapping young weasel at his side start to shake, he put his mouth to Zeke's ear and whispered his line: "I love you, Wendy Blackish." But although Zeke still wasn't able to repeat it, he wasn't the only one to hear it. Wendy did, too. And for some reason, hearing the words on Bagley's lips actually made her forget her embarrassment for a moment.

A blue jay swooped down over the crowd of weasels. As the flash of blue vanished among the tree trunks, Zeke coughed twice, trying to clear his throat. Even then he only managed "I love you, Wendy Blackish" in a hoarse, froglike croak. But at least he got it out. And when Wendy lifted her eyes to his, he grabbed her and kissed her.

A great roar rose up from the weasels, then everyone started to clap. The applause grew and grew, for the kiss was a long one. As far as Wendy was concerned, it more than made up for Zeke's little lapse.

That was all. The instant the kiss was over, the catbirds and mockingbirds, who had been watching the whole thing from up in the pines, burst into glorious song. They were very fond of the weasels, as are all musicians of those who appreciate their music.

Mr. Blackish danced the first dance with Wendy, but as soon as he handed her over to his new nephew-in-law, Zeke was his old self again. There hadn't been any dancing for a

whole, wet week. He was so glad to be back on the pine needles—and so relieved to have the ceremony over with—that he
finished the first song with a double back flip. He didn't do
doubles often, and for a moment he lost his bearings, standing
there feeling dizzy. But then someone took his paw, and as his
eyes came back into focus, he saw the wonderful weasel who'd
just become his wife.

"Another dance, honey?" he said, feeling like the luckiest
weasel on earth to be able to call her honey.

"May I lead this one?" she asked.

"Why not?" he said, not even making a face.

Only a couple of weasels had trouble entering into the spirit
of the festivities. These were Sally Spots and Mary Lou Silverface. Behind Wendy's back, they called her "that hussy
from the North Fork." Wendy had heard this, for the Wainscott woods wasn't a big place, but she was too happy to mind.
In fact, she'd hatched a plan for Sally and Mary Lou, one
that involved Ben and Bill Whitebelly. But today she just
wanted them to have a good time. So after three songs she
suggested to Zeke that he ask both his old girlfriends for a
dance. At this he *did* make a face, but he dutifully obeyed,
and as soon as he bowed in front of Sally, her scowl vanished.

Wendy had another motive for asking Zeke to dance with
someone else. She wanted a chance for a few more words with
Bagley, who was now standing off by himself near the stump.
She walked over to him and said: "Do you feel up to dancing?"

It was a question she would never have been able to ask in

the past. But now that she was a married weasel, some of her shyness was gone. Or perhaps it had to do with leading the way to the pond that day.

"Thanks," Bagley said. "But I think it might be a mistake to dance my first day up."

She smiled. "You don't like to dance, anyway."

"True—but with you I'd make an exception. I can't get over you sitting up all those nights."

"It was nice and snug, with the rain pounding on the brook outside. I never sat up all night before. I kept thinking—here I am in the den of Bagley Brown Sr., who made the Double B, and Bagley Brown Jr., who got the osprey nest off the telephone pole."

"Not quite matching accomplishments, I'm afraid."

"Oh, I don't know about that. Did you go through all that just to help your friend the frog?"

"Well, er, not exactly. I have another friend in the pond. Or, I should say, just an acquaintance, but . . . Anyway, things seem to have worked out beautifully, thanks to the rain—and all of you."

Wendy suddenly felt so fond of Bagley that she took his paw. "Thanks for helping Zeke with his line," she said, thinking how exciting it had been to hear them *both* say it.

But at the sound of throat-clearing nearby she dropped Bagley's paw. Zeke was dancing only a foot away with Mary Lou Silverface. Mary Lou was no longer scowling—but Zeke was.

"Husbands!" Wendy said, her eyes sparkling.

A PILE OF BUGS

The lower the sun sank, the louder the birds sang, and the more animated the dancing became. Soon Zeke sauntered over to reclaim Wendy. She went to whisper something to Ben and Bill, then joined her husband on the pine needles. In a minute or two, Ben drifted over and asked Sally Spots to dance. Not to be out-done, Bill asked Mary Lou. More and more weasels joined in. Even Mr. Blackish got into the party mood, waltzing Mrs. Blackish out among the younger couples.

Before long, there were only two creatures under the pines who weren't dancing: a rabbit peeping out from behind a sapling, and Bagley. Bagley slipped away. He'd done his duty as best weasel, and since he was still recuperating, nobody would be offended by his early departure.

Having just slept for a whole week, he doubted he would sleep very soundly that night. But he dozed off as soon as he got home, and when he woke up, it was the next day. There was sunlight—and an egg—in the entrance to his den. He walked outside, rubbing his eye, and found the sun already high in the sky.

After a late breakfast, he sat down on the bank. But staring at the brook just brought back his old envy of the water. If only he, too, could wind his way down to the pond! After all the rain, the end of the hollow log might be out over the water again.

But now that he knew everything was all right down there, he had no excuse for going. It would be a mistake to fall back into his old ways. And really, he had no right to mope. His great wish—that Bridget should be safe and sound—had come true.

After a while he lifted his eye to the dead limb over the brook. The dewdrops on the spiderweb had dried up hours ago. Now the only things caught in the silk were dead insects: over a dozen, it looked like. He crept out onto the limb and complimented the spiders on their recent handiwork.

"Mm, we're pleased with the new web," one of the spiders said. "We made the weave a little tighter this time. Seems to trap more bugs."

"Then you wouldn't mind if I took a few?"

"Help yourself," said the other spider. "Just be careful of the silk, if you don't mind."

Bagley carefully plucked out five dead bugs: a horsefly, a deerfly, and three houseflies. He stored them in his den, figuring he'd toss them into the brook an hour before the fish liked to feed. But that wasn't until late afternoon.

To pass some time, he went for a walk in the woods. There wasn't a soul around. At last, on the far side of the pines, he saw an old lady weasel carrying bits of eggshell out of her den.

"Where is everybody?" he asked.

She gave a little curtsy. Though he'd lost a bit of weight during his illness, there was no mistaking Bagley Brown, and she remained, like most weasels, in awe of the name.

"Well, sir," she said, "that wedding dance went on the whole night. At sunup a bunch of them went off to the Double B—bless your good father's memory, sir—and there was a big egg breakfast under the pines. I don't sleep so good myself, being old. But I don't expect many other weasels'll be up today at all."

The mere mention of sleep made Bagley drowsy again, and he returned to his den for a nap. He didn't wake up till late afternoon, almost time to drop the bugs in the brook. But when he took the five bugs out to the bank, he noticed some little white wildflowers on the opposite bank, flowers that weasels call wedding bells, and they made him think of Zeke snuggled up somewhere with Wendy—the sweetest, prettiest, bravest weasel imaginable. And here he was with a pile of dead bugs!

While brooding on how pathetic his life was, he heard a splash, and something inside him trembled open, like one of those wildflowers at the first touch of sunlight. Was it possible a fish might swim up the brook from the pond for a visit?

But, of course, this was absurd. It wasn't a fish. It wasn't even a bullfrog. It was a turtle, crossing from the opposite bank.

"Oh, hello," Bagley said politely, swallowing his disappointment. "How are you?"

"Not too bad," the turtle said in his slow drawl. "You?"

"I'm . . . I'm . . ." For some reason, Bagley couldn't seem to find any words for how he was.

"Sick?" the turtle ventured.

"Actually, I wasn't feeling too well. But I seem to be on the road to recovery."

"I'm afraid I'm intruding. I was just passing this way, and I remembered you said to drop by."

"Of course! In fact, I happen to have some nice, juicy flies for you. Which do you prefer—horseflies, deerflies, or house?"

"Hm. I wouldn't mind a horsefly, if you really have one handy."

Bagley got the horsefly, and the turtle came up and ate it right out of his paw.

"Delicious," the turtle said. "Thanks."

"How about a plain old housefly for dessert?"

"I've got a ways to go before dark, so I better not overeat. That's the great thing in life, you know, to travel light—especially when you have a heavy shell. But, well, maybe just one . . ."

After gobbling up a housefly, the turtle bid Bagley good-bye and started slowly up the bank of the stream. When he was out of sight, Bagley tossed the remaining three bugs into the water. He watched them float downstream. Two of them snagged on a stick poking out from the bank. One made it by the stick, but a little farther downstream a toad hopped from behind a stone and snapped it up.

Bagley didn't know whether to laugh or cry.

The sun sank even lower, and the rays filtering into the woods tinged the rain-washed leaves of the oaks with gold. The silk of the spiderweb caught some of the gold, too, and so did a small cascade up the brook. The Wainscott woods had never looked more beautiful. But none of the weasels appreciated it. Most of them were still sleeping off last night's festivities, and Bagley, slumped outside his den, was feeling too depressed to notice his surroundings. This time he didn't even hear the splashing in the brook.

The spiders did, however. "Will you look at that," said one of them. "Must have heard it's buggy up here."

"Weasels, turtles, and now *fish*," said the other. "Where will it end?"

Arriving just beneath where the weasel was sitting, the fish poked her head out of the water. "Bagley?" she said in her sweet, bubbly voice.

This he heard. But when he looked down, the slanting rays bounced off something shiny into his eye, blinding him for a second. He moved his head to one side. The shiny thing looked just like Bridget's head, her scales resplendent in the sun. But how could it be Bridget? She didn't even know his name.

"Bagley?" she said again—in what was unmistakably Bridget's voice.

"But . . . how—how did you get here?"

"Swam."

"But . . . isn't that dangerous? I mean, couldn't someone grab you out of the brook? Like a raccoon?"

"Well, I suppose. But not half as dangerous as climbing a telephone pole in broad daylight."

"How'd you know about that?" Bagley asked, more surprised by the moment.

"Everybody knows."

"Everybody?"

"Everybody in the pond. Paddy spread the news, I imagine. Bullfrogs aren't known for keeping secrets."

"But how did you know my name?"

She laughed her bubbly laugh. "Everybody knows your name. You're first in everybody's bedtime prayers. When Paddy told me this morning you were feeling better, I just had to come see you. He gave me directions."

Bagley wanted to shout for joy. But instead he asked politely: "How are the kids?"

"They're fine—thanks to you."

"It wasn't all me, believe me. And how is your, um, your husband?"

"Oh. You didn't know?"

"What?"

"The osprey got him. Two weeks ago."

"Oh, no!" He thought in horror of the heads he'd tossed out of the nest. Had her husband's been one of them? "I'm so sorry, Bridget. You must be devastated."

"Well, it was pretty awful. But so many were lost. We're just happy to have the whole thing over with."

"But your husband. You must be in mourning."

"Well, yes. Though I have to admit, we were never in love."

"You weren't! But you started a family and everything!"

"Maybe I should explain to you something about the way we striped bass have babies. We find a shallow place in the reeds, and the female sort of flops up on her side to force the eggs out, then a male comes along afterwards and fertilizes them. It's not all that romantic."

"Really," Bagley said, fascinated—and rather pleased. "So you weren't in love?"

"Not with him."

"Oh. With . . . someone else?"

She looked down at the water.

"You once told me that fish are meant for fish," Bagley said. "Do you still think that?"

"Well, I'm not really sure anymore," she confessed, looking up again. "The truth is, I was just spouting what I'd always heard. It's the inside of things that matters, not the outside. I see that now."

Bagley glowed inside. "Maybe . . . maybe we could start seeing something of each other again?" he suggested.

"Well, that's another reason I wanted to come up here, Bagley. Partly to thank you, with all my heart, and partly to say good-bye. Now that the pond level's up again, the human beings will be cutting it through to the ocean. They usually do it twice a year, to clear it out—once in the spring, and once later in the summer. Now that the kids are growing up, I'll be going out to sea."

"What? But you can't!"

"I'm afraid I have to. It's what we do."

"But if you're out at sea, I—we won't be able to . . ."

As his voice died away, the light began to dim. The sun had set.

"Uh-oh," Bridget said, glancing downstream. "I better be getting back. It'll be scary in the dark."

"You're—leaving?" Bagley almost choked on the words.

"I'm afraid I have no choice. But . . . are weasels better with secrets than bullfrogs?"

"I don't know."

"Well, I'll risk it. Could you come here a moment?"

"What?"

"Come here. I have a secret for you."

Bagley stepped down to the edge of the brook. As he put

his face close to hers, Bridget swam an inch or two forward and kissed him, a cool, tender touch on his cheek. Then she shimmied backwards and sank beneath the surface.

Crouching there on the bank, Bagley experienced the peculiar sensation of being warm and cold at the same time. Bridget's going out to sea was the worst blow he'd suffered since his mother's death. Yet her kissing him was a miracle.

But the cold soon won out over the warmth. She was gone! And he'd let her go without saying a word of farewell, just as the other time he'd failed to introduce himself.

"Bridget!" he cried. "Watch out for surf casters and their shiny lures!"

Could she hear him? He raced downstream along the edge of the brook, trying to catch up to her. But all sorts of stones and twigs crowded in on the little stream, forcing him to hop and scramble along.

Things were smoother once he broke out of the woods—and prettier, too. The potato field and the pasture were lush from the recent rain, and the brook between them caught the sunset so it looked like a rose-colored ribbon on a big, dark green package. But Bagley was running much too hard to appreciate the scenery. The sky and the brook were darkening by the moment, and there was no sign of Bridget. She was a fast swimmer in still water. With a current behind her, a weasel hardly stood a chance of catching her.

A truck was parked on the edge of the potato field, ready for the harvesting of the crop. As Bagley neared the giant thing, his legs buckled and he did a somersault, landing in a sitting position against one of the tires. For a moment the darkening sky turned jet black, and a roar like the ocean filled his ears.

Little by little, things returned to normal. He'd just been faint from overexertion. He must not have quite recovered from his week in bed after all. He sat there breathing slowly in and out. Off in the distance, beyond the potato field, an orange sliver of moon hung over the dunes. To the right, the Big Dipper showed up against the darkening blue.

After a while he felt strong enough to head home. But he moved only as far as a tuft of grass by the brook. It was a curious thing. Here he was, under the open night sky, but his heart wasn't pounding. Had the day on the beach and the telephone pole somehow cured him of being sky-scared? Maybe it was just that he had nothing much to live for, now that Bridget was going out to sea. Would she come back to lay more eggs when they cut the pond through next spring? It was possible. But, tongue-tied fool that he was, he hadn't even asked. Chances were, he would never see her again.

In his weakened state, the thought of this got the better of him, and a tear spilled out of his eye. First his parents. Now his dream.

Then something bright appeared before him, almost as if the sun had decided to pop back up for a moment. He wiped a paw across his face. Floating in the air less than a foot away was a tiny lantern, throwing off a greenish-gold light. It was a firefly—a lightning bug, as his father used to call them. Bagley had run across them before, but never from this close up. He could actually see the dirt on his paws by its light.

The magical lantern floated away and went out. Bagley stared after it. The firefly didn't come on again. It must have drifted around behind the potato truck.

Deserted again, Bagley watched the stars bud in the sky. It wouldn't be so bad, he decided, if the next creature to happen along was an owl, swooping out of the sky. But before long he heard some splashing down in the brook and got an unmistakable whiff of muskrat.

"I *told* you we wouldn't be able to make it home by dark," a voice complained.

"Because you're so slow," said another.

"No, it's because you're so greedy. You just had to go back for seconds."

"I am *not* greedy! It's just there's so much good food over by the bridge since the rain."

"Expecting to get there and back in ten minutes! Who do you think you are, anyway, the Wainscott weasel?"

"Did I say that? Though, if you want to know the truth, I bet I could get an osprey nest off a telephone pole, if I had to."

"When snapping turtles fly!"

Bagley sat bolt upright, wondering if he'd heard right. He'd automatically assumed the muskrat was referring to his father. Could it be they'd actually been talking about *him*?

As the muskrats drifted out of earshot, Bagley leaned back

on the tuft again. It wasn't so bad, really, sitting out here watching the tail end of the sunset without being sky-scared. As the last purplish glow died in the west, a cool sea breeze swept over the dunes and across the potato field and touched his face, bringing back Bridget's kiss. Their first and farewell kiss. But he refused to feel sorry for himself anymore. For, in a way, that kiss was sort of like the firefly. Brief as the magical glow had been, it had shone on him—right on him.

Maybe this wasn't much. But it was enough to light Bagley's way home in the dark.